I0589101

THE  BEHIND THE 

CHRISHANA GREER
CO AUTHOR: BROOKLYN DAVIS

CONTENTS

CHAPTER 1

Growing up in Chicago, especially on the west side of town, you never know where you might end up. Chicago was far from a fairytale, so I was exposed to a lot of things at an early age. From drugs, murders, and state prisons, I knew about it all. Chicago was a city that held well over 2.7 million people within it, but growing up on the west side of town everyone knew everyone. Therefore, Chicago didn't seem so big. Everyone knew me as Juelz's woman but my name was actually Ebony. I stood at 5'4, a sexy, mocha latte skin tone with thick beautiful hair weighing in at 140 pounds. I was every man's dream. My name wasn't trashed in the streets from dealing with so many different men, I had my own shit. I knew how to grind for mines by any means necessary, the legal way. Plus, I wasn't mixed up in drama. It just wasn't my cup of tea for my business to be in the streets, I was just "E."

I had worked my butt off in school. This enabled me to get out of my mother's house right after high school and attend Clark Atlanta University. I must say, Atlanta welcomed me with open arms. Living in Atlanta was a completely different living experience and environment from Chicago. Atlanta was the place to be, every night was a party! Whether it was day parties or night parties, there was always something going on in Atlanta. Typically, in Chicago when you attend parties, you had to be cautious. Someone might easily shoot up the party, or you could walk out your front door and become a victim of senseless gun violence. Someone getting shot and killed was a typical thing from where I am from, but not in Atlanta though. Danger was everywhere and being aware of your surroundings was always a must. But, Atlanta's atmosphere was different. The people were much friendlier. The air was fresher. The food was richer. Most importantly, the violence wasn't as high as Chicago. The feeling of being able to enjoy yourself at a gathering or something simple as a quick jog was calming. The feeling of not having to constantly look over your shoulders in fear of a car pulling up shooting randomly felt amazing. It was peaceful.

Don't get it twisted, Atlanta had its flaws too! Atlanta was also known for its killings as well. But, it wasn't with guns or anything of that nature. Atlanta was one of the top cities for the highest rate of HIV, and down low men. The feeling was incredible, not having to continually look over my shoulders in fear of someone randomly doing a drive-by shooting. However, I did have to be wary as to whom I chose to deal with when it came to men. If I ever did decide to date anyone while living in Atlanta. At the current moment, I wasn't trying to do anything but keep my head in my books, while partying at the same time, and talking to my high school love, "Juelz."

Juelz was a fine caramel latte who rocked a fade from time to time, depending on his situation in the streets and if his name was hot by the cops. Weighing roughly 165 pounds with the height of a basketball player, and the muscles of a MMA fighter with tattoos all over his body, he was everything. He was the finest thing hitting the streets in Chicago, and he belonged to me. My best friend Bri would always say, "E, he's not even that fine. Plus, this isn't high school anymore. You've outgrown him and he's not worth the drama. You're the breadwinner between the two of you guys, just remember that." I didn't care what anyone said about Juelz...he was everything in my eyes. Even though my paper was longer than his, it didn't matter.

We looked good on the surface, but Juelz and I were far from it. There was a lot that came along with dealing with Juelz. Insecurities, lies, deceit, women, money issues, etc. You name it, and I can bet you most likely we have dealt with it. Our current dilemma was me being in Atlanta while Juelz was back in Chicago. Often this caused issues between the two of us. But, regardless, we always knew exactly what our situation was. He was mines and I was his. There wasn't anyone who could tell me different.

At least that's what I thought, until school ended for summer break, and I decided to fly back home to Chicago. This summer break wasn't like any other trip home. This trip was about to open my eyes to something I was not prepared for.

From this trip I would soon learn the defined meaning as to what was the true meaning of love, loyalty, the value of family and friendships. It would all start with meeting someone name "KJ." That's when all the drama would begin and my life would suddenly changed. Here's how everything happened.

CHAPTER 2

Ring, ring.

"Ebony, have you seen the status on social media about you and KJ?" Bri screamed, as soon as I picked up. Before I could even respond, my cousin Tiara was flooding my phone with unlimited screenshots.

"Hold on, Bri. Let me read what Tiara just sent me." Social media was cool to post pictures and get the latest tea on what was going on. Whether it was relationships, who was messing with someone else's man, or sex tapes being uploaded, social media was the place for it. But that was never my image. I was the girl who set back and posted pictures to let everyone back home know that I was still alive and doing well. Brianna, better known as Bri, calling me about some social media nonsense that was the beginning of something new for me—especially if it had anything to do with KJ and I.

"Bri, Tiara just sent me some pictures of Raven talking mad shit on social media. What is her problem? Why the hell is she so mad? Most importantly, this bitch is my cousin. Why not call me, or call someone to get ahold of me, if there was a problem? She's talking crazy on social media, and there's nothing but peasants talking crazy like I won't pull up!" Screaming through the phone to make sure Bri understood me loud and clear.

Bri had never heard me get into it with anyone, but she knew my mouth was dangerous. I knew exactly how to hit, where it hurt, and then keep it moving.

"I had to call you because I know you deactivate your social media account often. I figured if you had not seen this post, then your page had to be deactivated.

Plus, as a friend, I couldn't allow anyone to sneak diss my friend without me informing them," Bri explained to me.

"Matter of fact, Bri, let me log in to your account. This thirst bucket wants my attention? I'll give her my attention. I'll call you back once I finish," I said requesting with blood boiling inside of me before hanging up the phone.

Within seconds, Bri sent over the information for her account. By that time, this weak-ass, attention-seeking post had over two hundred comments, all from bitches who were supposed to be my family.

"Raven, instead of worrying about KJ and me, you need to be worried about how you're going to see your kids when they are standing to the left of you." Then I did the symbolic mic drop and logged off.

Raven had a glass eye from a fight she had when she was in high school causing her to lose her vision. She was trying to help one of her "so-called" friends fight. She wasn't the most attractive young lady, as she was short dark-skinned and overweight. Raven and I were a year or two apart, but when it came to how we lived our lives, we chose completely different paths as we got older. Raven and the rest of the women in the family wanted to party, do drugs, have sex with guys for money, and bad-mouth anyone in the family who had anything going for themselves. I chose to go away to college.

This family had always been messy. Eighty percent of our family was made up of women, so of course, the messiness was destined to happen. But to make a post about KJ and me was a bit extreme, even for these messy bitches.

Let me provide you with some background knowledge as to who KJ was. I had met KJ a month after I decided to come home for summer break from obtaining my bachelor's degree. We kicked it off instantly. He had been trying to get me to allow him to take me on a date for months before I came home. He had been hitting up anyone and everyone, asking about Ebony. I had heard of him, but local dudes weren't my thing. After a lot of convincing, I finally decided to go out with him. Plus, he was kind of cute in his own little way. He was a chubby, goatee-wearing, 360-waves-rocking, chocolate drop. Don't get it confused; local guys never stood a chance with me. But he was an exception. Plus, it was only a date. It wasn't like we were going to start dating or anything.

CHAPTER 3

"Hey, beautiful. I am outside."

I read the text message from KJ, as I continued to look in the mirror to make sure my hair was perfectly laid. Even though, I had read his message, I continued to take my time coming out. KJ was a local dude who didn't say much. I could tell that he had a lot of women flocking to him from every direction. When females first saw him, they would instantly think of money, because that was what he looked like. Why not have him waiting? He was use to women running to him and being anxious for him. Mostly because they felt they could come up from dealing with him? He was about to learn how Ebony did things.

After twenty minutes of wasting time, I slowly glided out the door and walked toward his car.

"Ma, where do you want to go?" He asked. There were usually a few things that came along with dudes like KJ: drama, street beef, and baby mommas. Doing anything in the local area was out of the question.

"Let's hit up downtown. I am thinking Dave and Buster's," I suggested.

"Cool," he said, nodding his head.

The ride there was a little different from what I was used to. KJ decided he wanted to cruise on the expressway, blasting gangsta rap music. Now, I can't tell him what he can or can't play inside his car, but he sure knows how to make a good first impression, I thought sarcastically. The music was extremely degrading and not my style. Everything was "bitch this" or "kill this" or "kill that"— a little too hood for my blood.

After hearing the sixth song about how "bitches ain't shit," we finally pulled into the parking garage.

"KJ, have you been here before?" I asked as I closed the door of his white CLS Mercedes Benz.

"No, I don't really like to do stuff like this. I am more of the 'sit in the trap house all night while my girl is right there watching me gamble' kind of man," he stated, laughing.

I thought to myself, "Did he really just say that?" I laughed it off because he couldn't have been that honest and that stupid to mean it seriously. As we walked towards the main entrance, we were greeted by the doorman, who directed us in the direction to purchase the tickets and coins for the games. Dave and Busters was an arcade room where adults could eat, drink, have parties, and play games.

As we approached the receptionist to purchase the tickets to access the arcade, KJ had already pulled out a roll of money. I figured this was what he was used to doing, and he was trying to show me what he was holding a little cash. Little did he know I had my own money as well and stunting on dudes was my specialty. I let him floss with his roll of cash. I figured he had more singles in that bankroll than big bills. Also, people with money aren't required to pull out everything in their pockets (including the lint). I was going to stunt on him in a different way—a way he had probably never been approached when it came to his money.

We had begun to play a few of the arcade games. From the looks of things, this man was definitely outside of his element. It was almost as if he didn't know how to have fun. At first, I figured he was simply nervous and couldn't believe that I'd allowed him to take me out on a date. We had been here a good hour, and not once had he smiled. It was almost as if he didn't know how, as if he was fearful of fun. For a second, he had me thinking it was me. I was the life of the party of anything I was in attendance of and everyone who came in contact with me, whether they loved me or hated me. But, one thing they would agree upon was that regardless of how they might felt towards me, I always made them smile in some way, at least once. For this man to not even hit a smirk had me wondering, "What the fuck is wrong with him?" I have never been in the business of trying to figure out what was exactly wrong with a person, but with him, I had to ask.

"KJ, what's the issue? Don't you know how to have fun? You aren't use to playing games?" I asked in a joking, yet direct tone.

"Honestly ma, I don't normally do things like this. I haven't had fun in a long time. But I am having fun." He said while walking toward the air hockey table. "Maybe we should grab a booth and eat inside, instead of playing another game?" I said, entirely over the situation.

This day had to be the emptiest it had ever been at Dave and Buster's. The host had allowed us to pick our table. Truth be told, I wasn't that hungry anymore—I was kind of ready for the date to be over. It was getting late, and I knew Juelz would be calling me soon to see what I was doing and what time we were going in.

Juelz wasn't my boyfriend. We had just been dealing with each other for years. We first started talking when I was a sophomore and he was a senior in high school. There were a lot of reasons why Juelz and I didn't make it and couldn't be together officially. We both played blind to the fact of what was in front of us. Plus, Juelz still wanted to play around in the streets and between every female's legs, so I didn't give a fuck about being out with KJ tonight. Juelz and I had been dealing with each other for years, and not once did he ever try to put the time and effort into actually being there for me.

"Hey, how may I help you guys today? Can I start you guys off with some beverages and appetizers?" By how fast the waiter was speaking, I could tell that he was new and probably in training.

"Can I get a water with a lemon, sir?" I requested.

"Yes, ma'am. For you, sir?" He stumbled over his words as if he was nervous.

"A lemonade will do. Can I get an order of hot wings and fries?" KJ requested.

"Are you ready to order as well, ma'am?" asked the waiter.

"I'll take the steak, medium well. Thank you." I smiled while requesting my food.

"I'll be back with your orders. Thank you," the waiter said as he walked away.

While we waited for our food, we sat there without saying a word to each other. By this time, my dinner was ruined. Never had I gone on a date with some-one with such poor communication skills. Before I knew it, the waiter was coming out with our food.

"Sir, can you box my food to go?" I demanded.

"You aren't hungry, ma?" KJ asked, confused.

"I am starting to feel a little under the weather. Waiter can you bring the bill?

We might as well end this night early." I spoke while fumbling in my purse for my wallet.

As the waiter returned to our booth, I handed him my card before he even had the chance to give us the bill to look over it. "I got this, love. Keep your change in your pocket," I said, sitting there with the biggest smile on my face. I knew I had thrown him a curveball with refusing to allow him to pay for the meal. Even though it was something so small, you could tell he had never had a female downplay his money. That was what he liked about me; I could tell.

I was something he wasn't use to. He could see that I didn't need his money, and holding my own would have never been an issue if we ever did decide to have relations with each other.

Chapter 4

"Housekeeping," screamed the strong accent Hispanic woman as she banged on our hotel room door on the 12th floor. I searched for my phone to check the time and turn the ringer back on. Juelz rolled over and placed his arms around me, placing a soft kiss on my forehead. He usually only did forehead kisses when he did something really fucked up with one of his birdbrained females, so I knew it had to be something. It was 9:00 a.m.—too early to be dealing with Juelz's fucked-up ways and the shit that he did. Plus, I had just left my date with KJ a few hours before. It might not have been the greatest date, but if Juelz knew that I was out on a date, he would've probably pushed me off the roof of this hotel, found the female whom KJ truly loved, and try to have sex with her. Juelz was emotional like that, and he didn't make sense at times. I had gone years waiting for us to be together and for him to commit to me genuinely. Not once did he ever try to do anything.

Let the next bitch come along, and he would praise her to the world. Yet, he never acknowledged anything I had going on but always tried to take credit for my success and accomplishments. Why stay? At first, it used to bother me. Over the years, I figured out exactly what I was dealing with. I stopped expecting him to be there for me. We had two different kinds of love for each other. My love for him was crazy, and I knew the nigga' wasn't shit. I was down with anything to help him better himself.

Juelz had kids prior to us, and I accepted them regardless of how much baby momma drama he had. When he reached his low, where he felt like he had nowhere else to go, I stood firm for both of us. He wanted to be a barber, so I offered to pay half for his schooling to help pursue his dreams. Before I went away to college, we would sleep in cars, hotels, and motels due to him not having a place to lay his head, even though I could've easily gone home to my parent's house. There wasn't a limit to what I would do to show him that I had his back a thousand percent. A lot of the situations that Juelz faced weren't big issues in my eyes. Not having a place to sleep was on him. Yet, he was more than welcome to come inside my home whenever. The only thing was, that during this time, I was still in high school and Juelz had never officially met my parents. We would have to wait until my parents left for work in order for me to let him in the house. He never complained, and I looked forward to those hours spent with him. That was love or maybe I was just naïve.

Juelz's love wasn't exactly like that. I wasn't sure how much he loved me, or if he would ever love me the way I loved him. He said he did, yet sometimes it was hard to believe. Whenever I would be away for school, Juelz would go missing, not answering the phone for weeks. He would be back home living his life as if I wasn't a part of it. He wouldn't respond to text messages, check to see how school was going or ask if everything was going okay with me. But, when it came time for me to return home, the phone calls would come nonstop. He would act as if he was in love with me just before it was time for me to fly back home to Chicago. I figured he did this because he expected that I would spend most of my time with him when I arrived. It was as if his decision to ignore me and push me off for weeks wasn't an issue. It would almost feel as if his love wasn't genuine or pure. His love was more so along the lines of convenient love.

If we were ever to be together officially, I would never be the most important thing in his life. I knew he would never fight for me as hard as I fought for him. Even after all that, it still didn't matter when I was in his presence. I would feel as if I was with my best friend, my future children's father, and the man who knew me best. That wiped away all of the things he didn't do. The emotional attachment I felt for him was so intense that I wouldn't know where to begin even if I wanted to leave him. The feelings were so strong when I was with him, and after that, I could feel the loneliness that he placed upon me. It was the feeling of being defeated by whatever he had going on in his life at the moment.

Sometimes I didn't get it. We met when we were so young. Through the years, one would have thought we would've grown stronger, making him realize that I was worth the fight, worth his love, worth being the person to make him want to better his life. One would have thought I would have been the reason he wanted to do better not just for him, but for us. Unfortunately, I apparently wasn't good enough.

Maybe if he did find out I had gone on a date, he would feel the same way I'd felt for years. Knowing that he was still out partying with bitches as soon as I turned my back or went away to school would open his eyes to calm down. Maybe he would hurt like I'd hurt over the lies and disloyalty. Perhaps, Juelz knowing that someone else was getting my time would make him want to do right. Hell, who was I kidding? If I couldn't get him to care about me after all this time, the nigga wasn't about to start caring now. Juelz would know shit that had happened, regardless if it was true or false. Gossip was always the truth when it came to me in his eyes.

Even though KJ wasn't exactly my type, I decided to entertain him. He was a lot different from Juelz. Hell, after that forehead kiss of guilt that Juelz placed on me, KJ didn't seem so bad. I reminisced about all the shit Juelz and I had been through while sitting on the edge of the bed in a daze. I thought about the lies, hurt, mistrust, and the times he left me to defend for myself. The times he didn't come to my rescue, and the times he couldn't talk to me because he was with another bitch while I was away at school. I remembered the times he would walk out of my life without reason and left me hurting for weeks, and the times he fucked bitches I had known of. I thought about the bitches he'd lied about, and the times he knew my relatives had died and didn't call because we were not on speaking terms. All I could see was red.

"Bae?... E?" Juelz exclaimed. Before he got a chance to say anything else, I started hitting him on the top of his fucking head, as if he had just done this shit seconds ago. I kept punching him in his face until his stupid ass finally rolled out the bed and pounced up. "What the fuck is wrong with you?" he screamed. "Keep your fucking hands off me before I—"

I cut him off mid-sentence. "Before you do what, nigga? Exactly! Shut the hell up." I begin to walk towards the other side of the bed. "For years, I let you do whatever the hell you wanted. Not once did you think about me. Not once did you think about us! Nigga, I should—"

Knock, knock. "Housekeeping," it was the same Hispanic voice that had spoken thirty minutes ago. That was when I realized the nosey housekeeper was listening to our conversation, and I didn't need any witnesses if I killed Juelz.

"Lady, if you don't get away from this door, we're gonna meet once I finish with him," I yelled from across the room. "Now, back to you, Juelz. I am done with this shit. You don't get it, and you don't care!" My fists were balled up, getting ready to punch him again. From the look in his eyes, he didn't get it. To him, I was just tripping and being crazy. I turned around and walked away, shaking my head.

Without a sound, a word, a thought, I put on my clothes, grabbed my phone and keys, and walked out. We never fought. The only thing we ever did was argue from time to time, and even then, Juelz would blame me for us arguing. That was his reasoning for why we were not together. We never fought physically, but today I had reached my limit. Today was the end. Today was the day I wanted to see whether he truly loved me, loved us. Would he fight to keep me with him and work things out? With Juelz being Juelz, he let me leave. That was when reality hit. He would never care about me or saw what we could've been.

CHAPTER 5

It had been two months since I'd last spoken to Juelz. He never reached out after I walked out of the hotel room that day. It was just another slap in the face from Juelz. It was cool though. I took the situation for what it was.

On top of that, KJ and I had surprisingly, gotten closer. We had gone on a couple more dates since our first one. Honestly, he wasn't that bad, or maybe I was so stuck on Juelz that I needed a distraction from everything, and KJ was just that. We didn't argue as much as Juelz and I did. That was only because I wasn't attached. KJ bought gifts just because. He never went shopping for himself without bringing me back something. Even though I never asked KJ for anything, it was his initiative that got me. Out of all the years Juelz and I had been together, we had never bought each other anything for birthdays, holidays, or "just because" gifts. Hell, we had never been on an official date. We never met each other's family or spent any holidays together when I think about it. That always made me feel as if I was a secret and we hadn't progressed any actual growth over the years.

KJ was the complete opposite. His family welcomed me in with no problem. His mother would call me to see how I was doing. He had a brother and two sisters, and they had tried to befriend me from the jump. I'd never been the type to kick it with family. That was his family, so that was where their loyalty stood. Plus, I noticed from social media that every female he previously dealt with, his sisters felt the need to try to get under and befriend them. I didn't have time for that fake and phony mess. My patience for bullshit had been extremely short since I'd left Juelz. I would've probably hurt one of his sisters if they fucking played with me, so I avoided the situation altogether. I spoke whenever I would attend a family event with him, but that was it. They knew who I was, but I could tell his family was as fake as the Louis Vuitton bag his mother wore. Still, it was a change. It was the fact that I knew them, and they knew me. That was more than Juelz had ever done.

I had decided to stay home for a few extra months after summer break had ended and was now itching to get back into school. Even though I was a student at Clark Atlanta University, I couldn't face the feeling of being homesick. I spent tons of money flying back and forth, when I wasn't flying overseas for vacation in between breaks from school, mostly to be with Juelz. Now, with that part of my life over, it was time for me to remain focused and achieve my degree. I decided to transfer to Chicago State University. I would be the first person in my family to achieve a degree, so school was a major goal for me.

KJ was really big in the streets. Once he found out that I was trying to get back in school, he was all in, attending orientations, going with me to pick up my books, and making sure I made it on time to sign up for classes. Hell, he even sat through the entire orientation with me, and he also had the nerve to check me for texting while the teacher was talking. I never complained. It was sweet. It let me know that he cared, not just about me, but about what I was trying to accomplish. That was more than what I was use to from my last situation.

CHAPTER 6

The more time KJ and I spent together, the closer I got to him. It was ironic, because in the beginning, I didn't think he would stand a chance. Yet, here we were, only a few months in, and it seemed as if he was perfect. Literally every second of the day, he was attached to my hip, and vice-versa. I was sure I wasn't the only one who was hitting his phone, but as long as he knew the feeling was mutual and we kept everything drama free and had respect between each other, then we didn't have an issue. At least, that was what I thought.

Tonight was the big fight against Mayweather vs. Maidana. Whenever there was a big fight happening, my people would throw a party. We would come together to laugh, drink, smoke (if that was your thing), and eat while watching the big fight. Normally, I would be away for school, and so I would miss the fight along with the party. The chance for me to be in town to hit up my first big fight party in a while was a miracle and shocker. But, from the number of Tequila shots that were being taking, I could tell I wasn't the only person happy I was home.

Usually, I could hang with everyone when it came to drinking, but I was convinced these ladies were trying to drink me under a table. Before I knew it, the fight was over, and I was in my car doing 75mph on the expressway following KJ home. This wasn't the first time that I had been to KJ's home or stayed the night with him. Yet, I knew I needed to sober up. He didn't rub me as one of those dudes who would try to take advantage of me because I was drunk. I morally needed to make sure I was in the right state of mind.

As soon as we pulled up to his house, I parked my car in the back of his house. I sat there for a minute to gather my thoughts. The tequila was weighing in on me tonight. I hadn't even realized that KJ had opened the driver door to my car. He gently took my hand to help me out of the car and walk toward the three flights of stairs. I began to laugh randomly. The only time I got ridiculously silly was when I was intoxicated. KJ continued to hold my hand and walked me toward the stairs to enter the house safely.

Once we finally made it up the stairs and inside the house, I rushed to the bathroom. I was drunk, but I wasn't stupid. I knew that the quickest way to sober up was to let the bladder release itself. Good thing I used the restroom, because as I stepped out, I noticed his apartment was still completely pitch black from when we entered. I prepared to defend myself if KJ decided he wanted to jump out to attack me or whatever. "KJ?" I said somewhat softly; he shared an apartment with his brother, and I didn't want to be rude. Actually, I didn't want him to think I was the "Drunken Loud Chick." You know, the chick who gets drunk, and her true colors come out—the hood rat side. As I entered his room, I turned on the light within his room and noticed he wasn't anywhere to be found. I was tired and too tipsy to search for him. Instead, I made myself comfortable in his bed, still fully dressed.

KJ entered the room and began to take off my clothes, informing me that he had a hot shower running for me. The hot water touched my body, I became more and more sober. The water was what I needed, and I was now sober—at least, that's what I thought. Until I felt him grab my hands to keep me from falling to the floor as he helped me out of the shower. I didn't plan on going to KJ's house tonight. Meaning, I had no clothes besides what I'd worn there. Today must have been his lucky day, because he literally passed me the smallest pair of boxers he owned for me to sleep in. From the looks of things, it looked as if he'd had these boxers since his childhood days. This man damn sure wasn't a size small, but if he wanted to see how I looked with these boxers on, then he could see—just as long as he remembered not to touch.

KJ and I had been seeing each other for the past few months but we had never had sex. I wanted to get to know him as a person and allow him to honestly get to know me before any intercourse took place. KJ knew how I felt when it came to this matter and never pressured me into doing anything with him sexually, so me lying in his bed with damn near nothing on was when his self-control would have to come into place. Especially, since I was exhausted, because as soon as my body touched his bed, I was out for the count. Then I felt something moist going down the back of my spine. Of course, he was craving me as I laid in his bed with just a pair of tight boxers and a fitted tank top on. He couldn't resist me. Little did he know that he didn't stand a chance—or maybe it was me who didn't stand a chance. The more I tried to fight it, the wetter his tongue felt as he made his way to my juice box. He kissed on my inner thighs before giving me the full course of what he had in store for me. My body begun to shake, and my hands clutched the sheets. I was there and at my peak. Before I knew it, I moaned, "Oh, baby," releasing all of my fluids on the silk sheets.

He was ready to insert himself into me. "Where's your condom?" I asked, while pushing him back before he had a chance to place all of his weight upon me. The oral sex was cool, but I wasn't going to allow him inside of me unprotected. He jumped up immediately when I asked him that and grabbed his keys. "I'll be back." He threw on his jacket and sweats while rushing out the door. I wasn't exactly sure where he had gone to in such a rush, at 3:00 a.m., but like he said, he'd be back, and I'd probably be sleep.

Within ten minutes, he returned into the once again pitch black apartment. As he entered the room, I could feel his presence as he stood directly in front of the closet in his room, inches from the bed. He stood with his back turned for three to five minutes. I continue to lay in bed, never questioning what he was doing.

Suddenly, I felt him crawl back into the bed before I knew it his moist tongue had begun to lick around my vagina once again. This time he was prepared. He hadn't given me the full encounter as he had done before. I didn't complain because I was drained, and so I'd settle for some quick second-round five-minute head. Us going to sleep was not a part of his plans. Without a second thought, my vaginal lips were gripping his protected manhood as he inserted himself inside of me. He began to stroke until he exploded into the condom. Then he rolled over and held me as we slept.

The next morning, we joked and wrestled around in the bed before showering together. As he watched the water slide down my back, it hit me: I was doing things out of the ordinary. Normally, after Juelz and I had sex, I would get up and leave the next morning, if not, right after I showered. It was rare that we stayed together after sex. It wasn't that we couldn't stay those nights together. A part of me was tired of the staying in different hotels, the sneaking, the lying next to someone you loved but never feeling the love back. Yet, Juelz was still the man I cared for, and

I was only having fun with KJ. I knew that if Juelz came around and showed that he was willing to give us a chance with real effort, KJ didn't stand a chance. The only thing about that was, that in my heart, I knew Juelz would never come around if it meant he was the one who would have to speak up and address the problem to fix our issues. Here I was, still here, showering and joking with a man whom I had just met months ago, smiling and laughing as if I had known him for years. Strangely enough, I still wasn't happy. It wasn't him. Maybe it was me. Maybe I wished he was Juelz. Maybe I wasn't truly done with Juelz just yet.

CHAPTER 7

"Baby, you're pregnant," KJ said, with the most profound smile while smoking his cigarette.

"Listen here, KJ. I do not play pregnancy games, so we're not even about to play those kinds of games. Matter of fact, you wore a condom, so miss me with the bullshit." I wore the most serious look on my face as possible. Pregnancy was not something I joked about. I had never been pregnant, and even though Juelz and I weren't talking still, that was whose child I wanted to carry. The thought of joking about pregnancy scared me. I went to the nearest pharmacy and bought some emergency contraception pills. Hell, I knew he wore a condom. Then it hit me. He was standing by the closet for a lengthy amount of time that night. What if he'd trapped me? What if he poked a hole in the condom? This nigga was trying to be able to say he had a child with me. This dude was mad tripping. Thinking as I tried to remain sane to prevent myself from panicking. I bought two emergency contraception pills and popped them instantly, still standing at the pharmacy counter. I figured if some of his special sauce did slip out somehow, it wouldn't stand a chance against a double dosage. That was double the strength and double the doses to kill whatever might have gotten to my eggs in full force.

Instantly after the pharmacy situation, I blocked KJ's number. I was not feeling the kind of negativity he was trying to bring into my life. As the weeks continued to pass, I began to feel extremely tired and lazy. My appetite decreased, and the only thing that brought me joy was relaxing in my home alone with peace and silence. No phone, no company, no social media; just peace.

It was rare that I disconnected myself from the world completely, but this stomach bug had me feeling like everything except myself. I was sad, happy, and confused, all within the same hour. Regardless of how much I rested, I couldn't get over the stomach pain; it began to feel unbearable. My back hurt as if I had just lifted a five-ton car. After looking at the calendar, I realized I had an upcoming annual checkup, which was perfect timing. It would give me the chance to address the constant pain and sickness I was having with some quick antibiotics for this stomach bug, as well as medicine for the constant pain I was having.

I was too lazy to get out of bed, and so I laid there in bed, weak, until the day of my appointment finally arrived. Generally, I was always late for everything, particularly doctor's appointments or anything besides class that had to do with me getting up in the morning. This day was different. I knew something wasn't right, which meant I needed to be there on time and squared away. I arrived a few minutes before my scheduled appointment, and I could feel my stomach beginning to drop lower and lower, making me feel the need to sit in the waiting room chair bent over, balled up, holding my stomach until my name was called.

"Ms. Harris, follow me Ma'am," said the nurse from between the double doors. I gathered the last strength within me to get up and walk to the back to see the doctor. I didn't know what it was, but I knew that the doctor was going to rid me of my pain, or I was going to refuse to leave his office until he provided me with some kind of resolution. The nurse proceeded with the basic measures, checking vitals and asking questions. The only thing that stood out was, "Are you pregnant?" When she asked me this question, I instantly responded, "No." Yet, all I could think about was the joke that KJ had made weeks prior. I was so deep in thought that I didn't realize the nurse had stepped out. Finally, the doctor walked into his office.

"Hi, I am Dr. Bravo, you're here for your annual checkup and are experiencing stomach pain, correct?" The nice, clean-cut, polished Irish man said as he took his seat.

"Yes," I responded while holding my stomach the entire time. For some reason, I could guess his next question.

"Do you think you could be pregnant?"

I uttered, "I am not pregnant, so mark that off your list."

He asked that I provide him with a sample of urine to rule out UTI, bladder infections, pregnancy, and STDs.

At this point, I didn't care what the problem was, as long as the issue was fixed. I couldn't go another day of dealing with the excruciating pain. Pain medicines, were going to be my best friend, once prescribed. The doctor handed me a tiny, transparent specimen cup to fill. That wasn't going to be an issue because sitting here made me feel as if I had been holding my bladder for hours. There was a bathroom inside the room where I was being seen, so I didn't have to go wandering the halls in search of a bathroom. Easy access! Once I finished, I attempted to hand the nurse the clean catch specimen, who must have stepped back into the room while I was collecting my urine for these ridiculous tests. Instead, she refused to take the cup from my hand while requesting that I place the cup of urine on the counter. She informed me that she was going to do the pregnancy test first because it took only a few moments to get back those results.

I sat there with the darndest look on my face. Here I was, having extreme health issues. Yet, she decides she wants to do a pregnancy test instead of sending the urine down to the lab to get checked. I stared at the clock as the long hand of the clock hit the eight for the third time.

Suddenly, the nurse requested the doctor's attention, interrupting him as he typed on his computer. He stood at the counter for possibly thirty-seconds. "Ma'am, the results from the pregnancy came back. Congratulations, you're pregnant. I'll order you some prenatal pills and make sure you are getting plenty of rest," he said with the biggest smile of joy on his face.

I didn't know whether I should cry or respond at all. A simple "thank you" was all I could give.

CHAPTER 8

Days had constantly gone by and all I could think about was the fact that I was actually pregnant. I found myself daydreaming about the feeling that motherhood would bring upon me and the kind of father Juelz would be. It seemed is unbelievable Juelz and I were about to have our first child together. Juelz had wanted a child with me for years, but I never gave him one. In spite the fact that he was a dog, the timing was never right for us to have a child, and I truly couldn't picture myself bringing a child into this world without some kind of commitment amongst us. But, here we were, about to have our first child together. A part of me became happy about my pregnancy while the other part of me was in fear of the situation as a whole. I didn't know how to respond. Was I supposed to be happy, sad or afraid? I just didn't know. Then it hit me, Juelz and I hadn't spoken in a while. Well, today was the day for us to change that. Hopefully, our child would be our son, which he had been wanting for years. We were about to be a family. We might not have been the Joneses, but it was going to work for us.

Staring at the phone, I analyzed the same message over and over before finally working up the courage to press send. "Hey, we need to talk. Can you call me in a few?" Just like that, the message was sent. As I waited for Juelz's response, I found myself fantasizing about how our lives were about to change. Maybe I'd name my son Prince. Juelz sometimes went by that name. Prince Juelz Smith—yeah, I like that. We would sit and wonder about how our children would be and now we were about to see. Mostly, I thought about how life would be for us if Juelz had ever gotten out of the streets, left the bitches alone, and stood by me. Now that there was a child actually living inside of me, everything roamed through my head at once. What if he didn't stand by me or the baby? What if he wasn't the father I always imagined him to be? Would the baby bring us closer or pull us apart? Would the baby make him be in the streets more? Would I be labeled as a "baby momma," or would he let it be known that we were a family when addressed? Was he going to …?

My thoughts were suddenly interrupted by the vibration of my cell phone which I was still holding within my hands. Uncertain, my heart was now racing from the fear of not knowing how the conversation will end, I took a deep breath and proceeded to answer.

"What's up? I miss you so much," a baritone voice said from the other end of the phone.

After being in deep thought about his possible reaction and how he might take the news, I wasn't excited to relay the news anymore. "Hey, I am pregnant." I expressed straight to the point with no emotions behind it. The phone was silent for a moment. "Juelz?" I uttered with disappointment.

"Baby, we're about to have a child! Yes, I am about to have my son. We can name him Prince, and he's going to be like his daddy. Where are you? Come see me. Matter of fact, stay in the house. There is to much stuff going on outside, and I'd hate for you and my child to be in the wrong place at the wrong time." His tone of voice assured me that he was just as happy for the baby as I was, which was a relief. It temporarily suppressed any fears I may have had about becoming a mother.

Over the next few weeks, Juelz spent as much time with me as possible, rubbing my back, kissing my stomach, laughing, and joking. It was almost as if this baby had made him into the man I had wished for him to become for years. He was the man whom I had fallen in love with during my high school years and he was now the man I had dreamed of him becoming. He was trying his best to show me that he would be the best man that he could be for our family. I was pretty sure that there were women still lingering around, but at this point in our lives, things like that didn't matter, and I couldn't stress over the situation. I was carrying the child of my best friend, my future husband, the man I wanted to spend the rest of my life with. There wasn't anything or anyone that could ruin this moment.

We spent days in the house just lying in the bed and resting. He would hold me so tight, making me feel the most secure I had ever felt with him in years. I was safe within his arms. It was like I had fallen in love all over again. My life was perfect—well, the picture was.

My new classes were starting soon, and I would have obtained my degree this upcoming year. Juelz was being very supportive and protective of me. I had never seen this side of him before. But, I could admit it had begun to put me on cloud nine that I would be giving birth to a happy, beautiful child. There wasn't anything else I wanted or could dream of. There wasn't anything or anyone that could change my outlook on life. At least, that was what I thought. Until Bri called to meet up.

Chapter 9

Bri and I were best friends. We talked about everything, from each other's darkest secrets to the petty shit we did from time to time. Bri was also there with me at the party the night of the Mayweather fight. We hadn't really spoken to each other since or had time to catch up because she was always hustling. Bri was the friend who lived by the term "the grind doesn't stop." The girl would be doing hair during the day and selling weed off the phone by night. Plus, her dude Carlos, was one of the biggest scammers in Chicago. The nigga could literally scam you out of your last meal, if he wanted to. Regardless, of the lifestyle she lived, that was my girl. We had been friends since we were ten years old. In whatever life or path she chose, she knew I was always there and was a call away if she needed me.

We hadn't spoken in weeks. It was time to drop the baby tea on her. We met up at our usual seafood and cocktail spot on the rich part of town, where all the white folks would go for brunch and thirty-dollar cocktails. We loved this place because the facial expressions displayed on those old white people's faces as their mouths dropped when I pulled up in my Porsche Truck and Bri in her BMW X6 was priceless. Two young black women driving cars that easily cost over eighty-thousand, if bought brand-new off the lot. The fact that we knew we could afford everything that most white people could, made us laugh.

I walked into the restaurant wearing my over-the-knee Dior riding boots, Designer Frames, and $2,500 bag as if I owned the place. I requested a seat from the host but then noticed Bri already sitting at the bar, drinking her favorite drink, a Long Island Iced Tea. "I'll take a seat at the bar. Thank you, sir." I had spoken, while I walked over to Bri.

"Big booty Bri," I said, loud enough for only us to hear. Bri was the meaning of thick as grits. All the guys wanted her, and she may have even strayed off a few times, but she always made sure she went back home to her man.

"Waiter, can she have a shot of Tequila?" Bri requested from the waiter before I had a chance to properly sit down.

"That won't be necessary, Bri. I am trying this new challenge called no liquor for nine months." I made known while doing a slight giggle.

She looked puzzled, "Ok, what's been going on? How's school? How have you been? How're things with you and KJ?" She hit me with a hundred and one questions without giving me a chance to answer the first one.

Fuck it. I wanted to wait until I ordered my lobster before dropping my tea on Bri, but here we go. "Girl, I am good. Waiting for school to start soon. Until then, Juelz and I are relaxing and patiently waiting for the months to fly by so we can finally meet our little prince." I expressed.

She instantly choked on her drink. I could tell this wasn't what she was expecting to hear today. "Juelz? Baby? Bitch, I thought you and Juelz were done. How did you get pregnant? Fill me in on what the fuck is really going on! Matter of fact, waiter, let me get another round of Long Island. Fuck it—give me a pitcher." The facetious side of Bri was coming out, but I knew she didn't mean any harm.

I explained the situation and how everything had happened with Juelz and I. Bri replied, "Best friend, you know I love you. That's not Juelz's baby. You and Juelz were not dealing with each other for months. And out of all the times I've been pregnant and had abortions, the math isn't right. Weren't you dealing with KJ? I am going to assume that the night of the fight party, you and KJ got it on. Right or wrong? That's KJ's baby." Bri expressed now in a gallows tone.

Bri made me think back to that night and what KJ had said a few days after we had sex. It wasn't possible that this could be his child. He wore a condom, and I took two emergency contraception pills right after, to avoid the chance of this being his baby or me even becoming pregnant. There was no way in hell I could allow myself to have a child with a man I had just met months before. There wasn't enough pain in my heart from all the things that Juelz had done wrong to allow me to hurt him like that. To give birth to another man's child? It was Juelz's child, and there wasn't anything or anyone who could tell me differently.

Sitting here with Bri rubbed me a little wrong, and suddenly I wasn't feeling well. So, I told her I'd hit her up later and decided to leave the restaurant before I even had a chance to order my food. While walking to my truck, all I thought about was Juelz, the man I loved with every breath in me, the man to whom I had given years of my life. I couldn't hide anything like this from him. I couldn't keep such a big secret from him.

Tomorrow was my first doctor's appointment. That would confirm exactly how many weeks I was. This appointment was going to help me determine how I wanted to play the situation. Basically, it was helping me decide whether I was going to act like the KJ situation never happened and lived happily ever after with Juelz, or whether I was going to have to tell Juelz the truth and hope for the best. The entire drive home, I was deep in thought. Before I knew it, I had tears rolling down the side of my face. Juelz had called seven times. Tears still running down my face, I couldn't answer a single call from him. Lately, he'd been so concerned and protective, and he would surely hear the hurt in my voice.

After pulling into my driveway, I noticed Juelz's car. I wiped away the tears and got myself together before I walked through the doors and into the house. I knew he was about to be all over me, hitting me with a thousand questions as to why I wasn't answering his calls. After reaching over to my passenger seat to get my purse and taking one last deep breath, I got out of my car and headed towards my front door.

As I walked up the two flights of stairs, I was greeted by my child's father with a lovely welcome. "Why weren't you answering your phone? You had me worried. I was about to hop in my car and …"

I cut him off from his little rant. "Baby, stop waving your gun around. I didn't hear my phone. I am okay, just a little exhausted. Let's rest," I said while placing a gentle kiss on his lips.

"Girl, you'd better not go far with my child and not answer the phone again. Fathers have rights too," he joked. All I could do was laugh, because even though I knew he was joking; he really was excited for the baby—our baby.

"Seriously, baby, I am tired. Can you set an alarm to wake me up at 9:30 a.m just in case I sleep the remainder of this day away? I have a doctor's appointment in the morning," I said as I began to undress.

"You mean, we have a doctor's appointment in the morning?" He walked up behind me and kissed my neck. Then he turned me around and begun to help me undress. It seemed since I'd announced the baby to him, our sexual chemistry had grown to the next level. We found ourselves getting it on, wherever and whenever. For this particular sex encounter, the living room floor was our location. Juelz slowly placed me on the fur rug while beginning to tell me how much we meant to him. Whispering things like how much he loved his child and how he was grateful that I was the mother of his child. He felt like the part that he had been missing in his life was finally complete. Before I knew it, Juelz had inserted his unprotected self inside of me. It felt like we had been rolling around for hours until we both reached the point where we couldn't possibly go any longer. After we finished, he pushed his naked body against mine and held me as tightly as possible. My eyes began to water because of the one mistake I had encountered with KJ. Now my family was at risk.

"Baby, that dude KJ, you were messing with. Did you ever do anything with him?" Juelz whispered into my ear. I laid there, confused and trying to piece together how he had even known of KJ, or what would make him ask such a question. Then it hit me: Juelz knew how to find out everything, if he wanted to. Hell, some shit would be brought to him, and he would've gone months without ever saying a word.

"What did you say, baby?" I said, sounding confused.

He repeated the question in the calmest tone. "Did you have sex with KJ?" He said while still holding me as tight as possible.

I guess this was my moment to be honest. I didn't know what to tell him or how to tell him. Lying wasn't an option due to the situation. I was disappointed at the fact that I was lying here with the man I loved and having to explain to him how I'd fucked up by dealing with this one person, KJ, a mistake. Juelz and I weren't together when the shit happened. It was the fact that I had allowed something and someone to ruin something that we had always wanted to share together. It was a mistake on me to put myself in a situation such as this one.

"Yes," I mumbled.

"Did you wear a condom?" He asked, unwrapping his arms from around me and sitting up.

"Yes, Juelz." It was pure honesty, and I knew he couldn't knock me for that. I had told him the truth.

"Is this baby truly mines?" He said, in the firmest voice I had ever heard him display towards me.

I felt my heartbreak. Bri had made perfect sense of the situation. As badly as I wanted to say yes, I knew deep down we were not dealing with each other during the time frame of my pregnancy, and we hadn't had intercourse, not once, while on our break. "No, Juelz," I admitted, as tears flooded my eyes once again.

Usually, Juelz wouldn't have said anything, trying to hide and fix anything I did, to avoid it surfacing to the public that I'd done wrong. To make it seem as if I was the perfect person everyone believed me to be. This time, he wasn't going to be able to do that. I had only seen Juelz cry once before. This was a different cry. But, this was a cry where I started to notice and feel as if Juelz had actually truly loved me after all these years, regardless of him not being able to display it as much as I'd wanted him to. At this moment, I knew he was hurt; for once, he had felt the amount of pain I had been feeling for years. The feeling of disloyalty, betrayal, and not being good enough because someone else was able to give the person you loved for years what they wouldn't allow you to give them. The situation was fucked up, but for once I wasn't the only one hurt.

Chapter 10

After Juelz and I had our big blow up, I was back at square one. Only having to work up the courage to tell KJ that I was pregnant. Finally, I thought, Fuck it. What else do I have to lose? Juelz hasn't talked to me since our last conversation about the baby, so let me call this fool, KJ, to give him the news.

"Hello?" A surprised voice responded.

"Hey, I'm pregnant." I said, straight, direct, and to the point.

"You're pregnant? She's pregnant! That's my daughter you're carrying, trust me. I always wanted a daughter." He was eager with excitement. "Come here. I am on the block."

Unfortunately, I wasn't that happy or stoked about the news anymore. "Give me a minute. I'll be there in a few," I said, before hanging up the phone. Hitting KJ with this baby news, was hardest thing I'd had done in my life. Relaying the news wasn't hard, but the holding back my tears was. Here I was, experiencing my first pregnancy with a man I never thought I would give the time or day, let alone be forced to get rid of my first child due to him. I'd never believed in abortions because I knew my child would be with Juelz. That was the only reason why I wanted to meet up with KJ, to let him know I was getting rid of the baby.

I slipped on some clothes really quickly, because after speaking to him, I would be going back home to get ready for my abortion appointment I had coming up in a few days. I decided to drive in complete silence. As soon as I turned onto the block KJ was on, it was as if he had seen my car instantly from the corner because as I pulled up, I could feel him eagle-eyeing me while wearing the biggest grin ever. He walked over to my car and continued smiling, waiting for me to park the car. He rushed over to open my car door and gave me the biggest hug. He was so excited, kissing my stomach, and naming the child already. What he didn't know was that I wasn't keeping the baby.

"KJ, I am not having this baby, so yeah." Spoken as I removed his hands breaking the tight bear hug he was giving me.

Apparently, those words changed that smile on his face to a confused look. "Why not? I am not paying for an abortion. You are having my child. I want my daughter." He spoke.

I could tell this conversation wasn't going to go to well. I wasn't sure how I wanted the conversation to go, but I knew I was over the topic of being pregnant and talking about it with him.

Weeks went by, and KJ would text, "Good morning. I love you," almost every day. He also called a thousand times throughout the day. I couldn't allow myself even to believe that the love was real. There was no time frame on love, but I knew if it had taken me years to get Juelz to love me and for me to love him back, the love KJ was trying to say he had for me was nowhere near real or genuine. After numerous attempts to get a hold of me, I finally answered his video call. With the biggest crooked smile on his face, he was anxious to know about how the baby was doing, ensuring me that we would have nothing to worry about if I kept it. "If" was a long shot. The only man's child I ever wanted to carry was Juelz's. There wasn't anything anyone could do to make me change my mind. At least, that was what I thought.

A few more days went by, and KJ continued to call. Today was the big day. Today was the day I was going to get my abortion. I had never gone through an abortion before. Bri had gone through a couple abortions and miscarriages over the years, so I kind of knew what to expect. I mean, it couldn't be that bad. She would have an abortion in the morning and be back outside the next day, smoking and drinking like she hadn't killed her baby the day before. I figured it couldn't be that terrible. I had never gone to my first doctor's appointment to see how many weeks along I was; I figured I would find this information out doing my appointment for the abortion. All I could think about was getting the abortion over with. I slipped on some comfortable sweats, figuring this process was going to be a drag, so I might as well be comfortable doing it.

The clinic was a twenty-minute drive from me. I drove there while listening to the radio, to avoid thinking about what I was about to do. I had never truly be-lieved in abortions, but I was never put in a situation where I would be forced to get one. I didn't know whether I was supposed to cry, scream, or look at it as a relief. As I walked into the abortion clinic, everyone sat there depressed. This was not what I thought it was going to be. Truthfully, I didn't know what to expect. There were girls crying everywhere, and here I was, sitting there saying, "How long was this going to take?" I didn't know everyone's situation at the clinic, but their problems or regrets weren't my concern. My only job was to do what was needed to be done and continue on with my life as if KJ and this pregnancy never existed.

While sitting there, the thoughts of getting rid of my child became harder to process. I wasn't sure whether it was the constant crying or the guilt upon me about murdering a child. Hell, it was even going against my spiritual beliefs. I didn't know what to do, but I knew I needed this feeling and these thoughts to leave my mind instantly. The longer I waited, the more I thought. I found myself asking God for forgiveness for what I was about to do. I was killing an innocent child who didn't ask to be here, a child who even though wasn't made from love or intentionally on my behalf, it was still a child—my child, to be exact. Before I knew it, I had tears flowing down my face.

"Ebony, get it together," was all I thought while wiping my face with the tis-sues that sat on the coffee table beside me. I had to get this abortion. I needed it. It was going to make things right for me and put my life back on track. When it came to Juelz and me, things weren't going to be perfect but at least I wouldn't be pregnant. My mind had begun to play tricks on me. I could see a little child running towards me, wearing a bright smile, and screaming, "Mommy!" It was a child that I could love, and I knew would love me back, regardless of any faults I may have. This was my child, my blood, a part of me. I had to do what my heart and mind were both telling me to do. Before I knew it, I was running out of the clinic as if my life depended on it, and I never looked back.

CHAPTER 11

Months had gone by since my abortion escape. I was now six months along in my pregnancy and sitting alone in a doctor's clinic. KJ hadn't learned how to balance his street life and his parenting life just yet. That was kind of sad, due to the fact that he was thirty-nine years old. He had begged for this baby but had never attended a doctor's appointment. He never did anything when it came to the baby, besides disrespect it and allow those around him to disrespect his baby as well. Everything soon changed for me as I got farther along in my pregnancy. When I could no longer get an abortion, he started showing his true colors. KJ became controlling. He wanted me to be under him constantly, which was cool, but I needed my space from time to time. All he wanted was for me to be under him while he gambled for hours. I could sit down with him for a few moments, but hours? I couldn't see myself doing it.

After I was no longer able to get an abortion, the dates stopped and the disrespect began. KJ would send random messages saying, "Fuck the baby," and his primary focus was him and Niesha, an eighteen-year-old girl with a six-year-old son. So, of course, she was lost in life and had yet to grasp the concept of being a woman, let alone a mother.

I had found out about Niesha when I was almost five months pregnant, after I'd sent KJ to jail. I wasn't a big fan of putting the police in my business, but I did believe that when a man became physical with a woman, he needed to be caged up with other men so he could fight his equals.

The fight between KJ and I took place when I was four and a half months pregnant. I was still going out, partying, and clubbing with my friends. I wasn't showing just yet and was still in denial about my pregnancy Whenever I went out, I wouldn't drink or anything; it was merely having a good time with my friends. KJ had an issue with me going to the club. Now, I don't know whether his problem was with me being pregnant and clubbing, or whether it was because anything could happen. Or was it the fact that my stomach was still as flat as it was the day he'd met me, and he feared I'd get someone else's attention? Regardless, all he had to do was express himself to me, so that I could have had an understanding as to where he was coming from.

It was just like any other Friday night. Diana and I were getting ready to hit up the club. Diana was a high school friend of mines, and each weekend we would get up and enjoy life, if she had a babysitter for her kids. Usually, we sat in our sections, popping bottles, dancing, and turning up whenever we went out. With me being pregnant, popping bottles wasn't anything that I could participate in at the moment, but there wasn't a rule that said women couldn't go out and have fun while they're pregnant. Diana and I had gone out to the club and were partying in our usual section inside of Club Vertigo. On this night, KJ hit me up, saying he wanted me to go in. I figured he had never simply hit me up randomly, telling me to go in the house, so maybe he had a bad feeling about the situation and me being out. I texted back "okay," hugged Diana, and told her I had to go.

As I walked out of Club Vertigo and handed the valet driver the ticket to get my car, while waiting I decided to call KJ to see what was the reasoning behind him wanting me to go in. "Hey, what's up? What's wrong?" I asked with concern.

"Yeah, I wanted to go to your house instead of mine tonight, and I was ready to go in," KJ said in a soft voice. Deep down I knew I didn't want a child with KJ. However, I figured, at least, I had to give him a fair shot at parenting and give us another try since I was going to be stuck with him.

"Okay, I am on my way home," I said before hanging up the phone. Valet had pulled my car to the front of the club. I tipped the valet driver and proceeded to drive home.

I had to be maybe thirty minutes away from my house before KJ video called again asking where I was? I informed him that I was still driving home, and he told me that I was taking too long; meaning that he would simply go home. I was not about to hit the dash and get pulled over by the cops due to rushing, so I said,

"Okay. Wait, KJ. Where are you?" I could tell that he was sitting in a car, and I needed to know exactly where he was and why he was there.

He took a slight pause, almost as if he had to gather his thoughts before he responded. "I am sitting on Central Park. I just finished gambling. That's why I called you, so I could decide whether I should go home. But, I wanted to come to your house instead."

Not thinking anything of the response, I said, "Oh, okay. Well, you're not coming over, so call me when you get home, or I'll call you when I get in—whichever comes first." I hung up.

Because KJ wasn't coming over, I wasn't in a rush to get home. It was 12:30 a.m., and I'd seen a twenty-four-hour Wal-Mart nearby. I had decided to stop and get a few things. I wasn't in the store for more than ten minutes before KJ called again, asking the same question. "Where are you?" I wasn't in a rush anymore; he had said he wasn't going to come over. After spending an hour in Wal-Mart, I finally arrived home. I pulled the car into my driveway and sat there for a moment. The thought of taking the bags up the stairs hit me. After a few seconds of sitting in the car, I gathered my bags out the trunk of my car and headed into the house.

Maybe forty-five minutes went by before KJ called again. "Hey, what are you doing? Are you home yet?" He seemed concerned.

"Yes, I am home and doing laundry now," I responded.

"Open the door," he insisted.

"Wait, what?" Before I had a chance to complete my sentence, there was a pounding on my front door. "Who is it?" I yelled from my room.

"It's KJ. Open the door," he hollered from the other side of the door.

I stood there in shock while opening the door. I didn't have a problem with him coming over, but it felt as if he was trying to catch me in the act of doing something. It was almost as if he was hoping to find someone here, given the way he paced through the house, checking behind doors, and opening closet doors. "KJ, who are you looking for?" I giggled as I stood and watched him pace through the house like an idiot. Lately, I had been feeling like he was insecure and becoming controlling. This was too much, even for him. I laughed in his face. "Baby, you missed a closet. Did you find who you're looking for?" I said in the most sarcastic voice while standing in the middle of my living room floor.

"You think you're slick. I heard you on the phone with some dude, because he had the phone on speaker. I opened the downstairs front door for him and everything. He was coming in your house!" He hollered while checking the pantry closet.

I found his allegation quite comical. "So where did this mystery man go? Did he run out the back door? How did he look? What did he have on? Was he cute? Did he have muscles? Is he under the bed?"

My remarks and laughter made him feel as stupid as he looked. "But I saw him. I saw you get out of your car. I was waiting outside of your house for an hour. I saw you carrying the bags. I saw when you put your key into the front door. I know what the hell I saw." He was sure he'd caught me in the act of something.

"Wait, what? You were outside my house for an hour? Why did you act as if you were at home? So, you were outside my house when we just spoke? Why didn't you get the bags out the trunk, if you saw me carrying bags? Stupid, there's no one here." I was irritated with the entire situation, and I walked back to my room and continued to fold laundry.

KJ must have realized that his actions were a little off the wall and made him look like an imbecile. He proceeded to the bathroom to shower. All I could think about while he showered was the fact that I had never had anyone pop up at my house, watch me go inside my house, and sit outside my house for hours. This shit had me feeling uneasy! It had to make him feel like an asshole as well, because after his shower, he helped fold the rest of the laundry and laid across the bed to go to sleep without saying a word.

I could've slapped the shit out of him for being so damn stupid, but I figured I'd leave the situation alone for the night. I took a steaming hot shower and headed to bed.

The morning was like any other morning, except for the fact that I was still bothered by KJ's allegations. I remained cool and acted as if nothing was bothering me. KJ could tell I was pissed at how stupid he was from the situation that taken place just a few hours before, so he slept under me, as if he was trying to hold me captive. While lying there with my phone in my hand and surfing the web, I got a video call from Diana.

Most people who had something to hide would have ignored the call when their mate was around them, and I could sense KJ, who had now awaken, peeking over my shoulder to get a glance of the caller ID. After removing his arm from around me, I rolled over from my side, in place my head directly on his chest, and answered the call.

"Diana, what's up?" I said in a calm voice.

"Girl, the club was popping after you left. Remember the tall guy you were standing next to in our section? Well, you know every time we go out, there is always unlimited bottles guaranteed. But he took unlimited to a whole new level last night!" Diana said in a humorous tone.

"Damn, she's ugly," KJ uttered disrespectfully in the background. Luckily, Diana hadn't heard his childish remark. She continued on with details as to what took place after I left. As well as her plans for the night. She figured I wasn't going out, and if I were, I'd hit her up later to let her know at the last minute.

KJ must have assumed that because Diana was calling me about the club, I was going out to the club with her tonight as well. That really wasn't the case tonight. Even though I wasn't showing and still had energy for the moment, I realized that I was pregnant and still needed to rest and relax. Regardless of how much in denial I was. If KJ would have asked me whether I was going out, he would've have known I wasn't. Instead, he began to scratch his nails down my thighs, which to the point where they begun to turn red. I ended the call with Diana mid-sentence. Before I knew it, KJ and I were wrestling in the bed. This must have been his way of trying to play or make up for being stupid and rude these last few hours. At least, that's what he portrayed.

KJ picked me up at the waist and sat me on his shoulders. He joked about oral sex by saying, "Oh, I haven't sat you on my shoulders yet and given you head like this yet, right? Let me put you down." He gently placed me on the bed. He then placed his hand around my neck. At first, it was playfully, but when I uttered that I couldn't breathe due to his hands tightening around my neck, he stated, "I know."

This wasn't his way of horse playing with me—he was literally trying to harm me. Was he mad that I had gone out the night before? Was he mad that he'd supposedly heard a man on the phone with me who somehow disappeared once he showed up at my doorstep unannounced? Was he trying to instill fear in me? Whatever it was, this wasn't the moment to figure it out. This was the moment to defend myself and get this fool's hands from around my neck. For the first time in my life, I had to fight someone who I felt could have actually cared about me at once upon a time. I had been dealing with Juelz for years, and we never got to a level where he put his hands on me. Juelz might scream and make threats, but actually hitting me wasn't in him. Yet, here I was in a situation where I was forced to fight, forced to protect myself from the man whose growing child was inside of me.

As he squeezed tighter, my arms swung faster and faster, striking him in the face multiple times until he released my neck. Finally free, I jumped off the bed to stand toe-to-toe with him. His fist balled up, and he barked, "Hit me again!"

My fist balled up as well, ready for him to swing. "KJ, get out of my house."

He slapped me. "I am not going anywhere. You are going to have to call the police to get me out this hou—"

Before he was able to finish, I struck him in the face, causing blood to leak from his mouth. I didn't know what kind of women he was use to, but I wasn't one of those females who'd let anyone put their hands on me without trying to defend myself.

"Don't worry about it. I am about to call the police!" He screamed while reaching for his cell phone. "We are both going to jail. You see my face? They are going to lock your stupid ass up too!" He yelled, while dialing 911.

I stood there in disbelief. I wasn't worried about the police, but when I saw him put the phone up to his ear as if he was making that call, I figured I'd call too, if he felt the police were needed to defuse the situation.

"Hello, what's your emergency?" The operator asked. Before I had a chance to respond, this fool was coming back into the bedroom from the kitchen with a knife, screaming for me to stab him.

"Hello, ma'am? Are you okay? What's going on? I am going to track your location and send a car," the concerned voice on the other end spoke as she heard the commotion in the background. Before I knew it, KJ had run out the front door, and the police had my entire building surrounded by police cars.

This shit was new to me. I had never gone through anything as crazy and childish as this. Juelz and I knew our limits and never let shit get this far. I mean, why the hell would you want the police in your business? Basically, KJ wanted to play, "Let's see who could call the police first." This shit was crazy and had me boiling on the inside. I had officers at my front door, taking pictures of my neck. I hadn't even realized I had any marks on my body until the officer requested a picture of them. This shit was too much!

After everything was said and done, the officers wrote up the domestic violence report and told me they'd put a warrant out for KJ's arrest. I was over the situation and nodded as I closed my door.

A few days had gone by since the fight, and I guess the officers finally got hold of KJ. Which was the reasoning as to why later on that night, I got a call from the Dupage County Jail; supposedly, there was another call placed by his son's mother, of him following her car. What was so crazy about this shit was when they picked him up, they picked him up in Niesha's car. This was messy. He was calling for me to go to court for him and everything else. But before he was able to get deep into his conversation, Bri sent screenshots on KJ's social media account, with Niesha claiming KJ as her baby's father. So here I was, pregnant on a jail call with the man I was pregnant by, who's in jail because he wanted to see who could win in a one-on-one match between him and a pregnant woman. Now, this Niesha shit was coming up. I guessed Niesha was desperate to prove that she was dealing with KJ and having sex with him, that she sent out a sex video of KJ giving her oral sex in order for it to get back to me. All this, and for what? If she wanted him that badly, she could have him. From the looks of these screenshots, I wasn't the only female that she was focused on when it came to KJ.

"KJ, who's Niesha?" I said, cutting him off from his "I was just playing," rant.

"Who? I don't know a damn Niesha!" He yelled from the other end of the phone.

From these screenshots, I knew everything I needed to know about the girl. She was eighteen, and KJ was thirty-nine. That was how I knew she had a son. Hell, the screenshots Bri sent over told me everything about the girl except her social security number. She was young, immature, and believed anything KJ told her. She didn't know any better from the shit she posted online. From the screenshots being sent, she knew who I was, but I didn't know her. KJ had always had a crush on me and wanted my attention, so he would post me as his Woman Crush Wednesday every week or tag me in something to get my attention via social media before we started dealing with each other. She asked him about who I was, he told her we'd grown up together. I didn't get how she could be so dumb to believe that! I was sixteen years younger than he was. That was when I realized she was stupid and one of those females who believed anything the dude she was fucking told her. It was sad, but so was she.

"E, are you coming to bond court for me in the morning?" KJ asked.

I paused with the most confused look on my face. This man was really asking me to go to court for him when I was the reason he was in jail? That was when I knew he was crazy! "Call Niesha. Bye." I hung up before he had a chance to respond. KJ called maybe four more times that night, and each time I declined the call.

A few days went by, and Bri was sending screenshots still. Apparently, this Niesha girl had told someone that KJ had to be in jail, and that was why he hadn't called her. She was going to reach out to me so that we could go to the county jail, once she figured out which county jail he was locked up in, so he could see us both together. This girl was stupid and didn't have a lick of sense, if she thought I was about to waste my time visiting the county jail—especially to go visit the man I put behind bars. She let social media know that regardless of whatever he told her about me, she was still going to be there for him.

Even though she knew I was pregnant, she didn't care and had decided to get rid of her baby because she couldn't have a baby by someone who already had a baby on the way. I didn't understand it. She would get rid of a child because of the person she is dealing with having another child on the way by a woman who didn't know she existed? Yet, she'd continue to sleep with a man who was in a relationship with the woman who's carrying his child? The bitch was stupid—there was no other way around it.

In the midst of all the text messages that Bri had sent me, there was a light knocking on my door. No one knew where I lived besides KJ, Juelz, and some close family and friends, but everyone knew I wasn't with the "popping up at my door" games. The only person I knew to do this was KJ. And behold, that was who it was. KJ stood on the other side of the door looking like Inmate 2567.

I cracked the door. "KJ, what do you want?" I was confused as to why this man was at my doorstep and not in the county jail.

"Because you're my damn woman. Now, can you open the door? I am hungry and need to shower." He pushed his way through the cracked door, acting as if nothing had happened. It was as if he hadn't realized that he had been locked away for a few days for being stupid, as if we weren't just fighting like wild animals. He was crazy, and I knew I had to leave him alone—but not before addressing one last thing.

"KJ, I have a surprise for you," I said, smiling.

"What's up, baby?" He smiled, as he dropped his light blue Pelle Pelle leather coat on the floor.

I decided to message Niesha to get down to the bottom of things. "Hey, what's your number? You want to talk to your man?" I told her via social media while stalling KJ on the big surprise I had in store for him. Within moments, she responded with her number.

"Hold on, KJ. Let me make this call before the surprise." I was still wearing the biggest grin. I called her up. She had to be waiting for my call because she answered on the first ring.

"Hello?" A deep, unattractive, bashful voice spoke.

"Hey, girl. You want to talk to your man? Here he is." I passed the phone to KJ, but not before putting the phone on speaker.

"Hello? Who is this?" He said, confused.

"KJ, so you got a whole family? You got a whole girlfriend? You got a whole other life?" The breaking, manly voice trembled on the other end of the receiver.

"What the hell, do you mean whole life? What you thought I had, half of a life?" he yelled. Of course, I knew KJ was trying to avoid the situation and had to react quickly to attempt to gain control over the situation. I wanted to see how he was going to respond, and believe me, it was like a guilty person who had been caught red-handed. No need for the back and forward on my phone.

I delivered the million-dollar question. "KJ, who is your woman?" I asked, still laughing. KJ could tell I was being an asshole and finding this situation quite humorous, which it was. He also knew he needed to watch his words and how he responded in this situation.

"I am standing here with my woman. Anyone else is nothing to me." Damn, I didn't expect him to be so blunt with her like that—straight to the point. But that was what he was supposed to do. There wasn't any other way around it. Pick a side and stay there, and he picked the right side. But, what he didn't know was that I had another surprise for him.

Before hanging up, I could hear Niesha's heartbreak while she screamed, "Y'all belong together!" It had to hurt to listen to the person you're sleeping with and obsessed with telling you that you're nothing to him, in order to secure another woman's feelings and thoughts. This kind of reminded me of Juelz, even though

Juelz had never been put in a position like this. I felt her pain. Even though she was a dumbass I knew how it felt to care about someone who didn't defend you. I could relate to her pain on that level. On the other side, the feeling of having someone defending the relationship when need be, was everything that I had never gotten from Juelz.

At the end of the day, I was a woman, and so that was why my next surprise for KJ was well suited. "Hey, KJ, get the fuck out of my house!" Demanding as I walked out of the bedroom to pick up his coat from off my living room floor, directing him towards the front door just moments away from slamming it in his face.

"What? Ebony, your ass is tripping? All because of that bitch Niesha!" He said, outraged.

"No, nigga. It's because you put me in a situation like this, where I have to address another bitch about you! And what the fuck you thought I was over that fight? Bitch, you fought me while I was pregnant! You fought me period! What if I would have lost my child? You don't give a fuck about me, and you damn sure don't give a fuck about this baby! So, if you can shit on me, the person who's carrying your child, then I know you'll shit on this baby. Get the fuck out, unless you want to go back to jail! I am pretty sure your bond agreement was to not have contact with me, so nigga, lose contact!" Screaming as I stood opening my front door directing KJ to leave.

"Ebony, you gonna regret this! I am going to have my sisters beat your ass!" He screamed while I finally released the door in his face.

"Yeah…Yeah…Get the fuck out." I said as I walked back towards my bedroom. It felt great not having to deal with this nonsense. Things could have gone left instantly, but you don't put your hands on me and walk in my house like everything is all good. He had lost his mind. I was done with the situation, and I was done with him. But for some reason, Niesha still made me a factor in their lives, even after I let him be free to return to her, and whoever else to deal with the fist-fights that came along with him. One thing about street dudes, was that, you'll never be the only one trying to be the only one within their lives. Niesha hadn't realized that.

C HAPTER 12

After the whole KJ, Niesha, and me thing happened, I still remained the topic on all of her social media accounts. Niesha was one of those girls who loved to send threats and bark on social media without tagging the target in the post, knowing damn well the target couldn't see any of it. I mean, what other way was there for me to think about the situation? I was the highlight of her life. My child, KJ, and I were the topic of her page for months prior to me finding out about her. Hell, I wouldn't have even known she existed if it wasn't from those screen shots. She was just another out west, minimum wage working, still living at home with their mother and five other people in a three bedroom apartment, living off welfare ass female. I couldn't even take her serious or KJ serious on that note. She was lost in this big world and hadn't yet figured out what it was like to be a true woman.

Bri had sent me more screenshots of her making my child and I the topic of her social media page, saying shit like, "Oh, I'll spit on her, him, and their baby," and, "I'll stomp that baby out of her." We all knew I didn't do disrespect, and I didn't do slick talk without action. Threats were never my thing. I texted Bri back and told her to let me log into her social media account to see what was up for myself. One thing I had learned from Juelz was how to find out information if I really wanted to know something. I decided to check out her page in order to see what else she had to say about a woman she had never met. I found out that she was still dealing with KJ after he disrespected her for me. She knew exactly who I was and continued to make numerous posts about my child and I for months prior to me finding out about her. The young bitch had even made a status update saying "I hoped the baby dies. I didn't give a fuck about him, her, or their baby."

Even though I was not dealing with KJ, I still brought it to him. I mean, this was his child, and as a parent, it was your job to defend and protect your child against anyone. Instead KJ defended Niesha. He would always tell me that she was nothing to him. Which I didn't even care what she was to him because we were not together. But, I wanted to know, what exactly was his plan when it came to putting this girl in her place for disrespecting his child. He didn't have to defend me, but at least defend your child, regardless of who the person was.

I didn't get it. Cheating when we were together was one thing. That's something I could get over. We didn't work out, cool! Let's move on from each other's lives, yet still be able to coexist for the sake of our child. But, what I could not process was how could he lay down next to someone who didn't know me physically or had never seen me but was willing to disrespect his child because of some shit he did? Then, when I addressed her, KJ had the nerves to tell me to leave him and her alone, and to go find my child a father. Like the bitch wasn't the one who begged me to keep our baby. I knew I wasn't ready for child, especially with him! If he only knew how much I regretted getting pregnant by him every time I thought of him. When I thought about him fighting me, especially with our baby growing inside of me, I hated him more. I hated myself more for allowing myself to have a child by such a coward of a man. I knew deep in my heart that no matter what Juelz did, that was whose child I had wanted to carry, and that was the person I wished was my child's biological father.

KJ was turning out to be everything except perfect. He was untrustworthy, manipulative, conniving, deceitful, disloyal, and abhorrent. Most importantly, he was a snake. When we could find the strength within ourselves to have a civil conversation pertaining to anything, from the baby to general topics, he would screenshot the text messages conversations and send them to Niesha. He let her know when my doctor's appointments were, which I found interesting because he had never even attempted to make it to an appointment himself through out my entire pregnancy. He'd never been part of an ultrasound appointment. He'd never heard the baby's heartbeat. He was a deadbeat. Even though the baby wasn't born yet; he had already displayed the signs. He would record conversations we would have about the baby and send them to her. He had girls playing on my phone. He gave out my home address. He would send text messages saying he had females riding around multiple cars deep looking for me. I didn't get the point. Had he forgotten that I was carrying his child? He was not to be fucking trusted! He was immature as fuck for his age.

Everything that girl posted came from what he told her. The funniest thing she posted was, "My nigga can't fuck with a bitch that plays police games," and, "He told me about the nigga he caught in your house." She was referring to KJ's mystery man, leaving out the part that when he bonded out, he came directly to my house. The mystery man comment was just that: a comment. Did she see the dude in my house? Did KJ see him? KJ sure went to bed at my house that same night, but supposedly there was a man there. Let me guess: he was under the bed? I laughed at her post because she was one of those females who acted as if she played the game, but in reality, she was a puppet in KJ's circus. It wasn't worth addressing anymore, but it did make me realize a lot about KJ as a person. He wasn't a man—he was a bitch made-ass piece of shit.

So here I was, pregnant and going through it alone. My child's supposed to be father was taking care of a minor and playing step-daddy to her son while disrespecting his own. After a while, the words stopped bothering me. If I ever got my hands on Niesha, especially after she had wished death upon my child, I would have beaten her into a bloody mess. She wasn't really to blame, though—KJ was. He was the person laying down with someone who didn't have enough respect for him or his kids. He would never see his baby because of the lack of respect and his inability to be a parent. He was a mistake, and I was aware of that. Even through all that, I didn't complain. I was blessed. My baby was growing fine, and Juelz had managed to come back around for the baby.

CHAPTER 13

Juelz had came back during the beginning of my third trimester. He was there for it all, well, at least to the best of his ability. He would rub my stomach and kiss it every night before we went to bed. There were days when he wanted to stay out late, but he would come in to help me clean and make sure I was okay. Honestly, he made me forget KJ was even my child's father, which wasn't hard to do. The active baby moving around in my stomach loved when Juelz came around. The baby's little hands and feet would kick nonstop whenever Juelz was around. The moment Juelz laid his hands on my stomach, my stomach would begin to move with nonstop excitement, as if the baby knew he was near.

Even though Juelz was there for me, I knew he was hurt. I could tell by the way he would look at me. The amount of pain in his eyes was unbearable. It was unreal. I knew it was only a matter of time before he would no longer be able to pretend as if this matter wasn't hurting him. It was as if he was feeling what I had been feeling since the beginning: the feeling of emptiness. Of course, Juelz still played in the streets with bitches, but now it was different. It was like he did more and more drugs each night and entertained more and more women as a temporary pain reliever from the reality of me bearing someone else's child.

The months went by with Juelz being around, and then one day he asked straight up, "Why didn't you get rid of the baby?" I had known the topic was going to come up eventually, but not this soon. At the moment when the pregnancy was fresh, Juelz had vanished; that was his way of dealing with the situation of my child not being his. He left because that was what Juelz was known for. I had no clue Juelz was going to come back around and be a part of my life, or stick around for my pregnancy.

Plus, during the beginning, KJ was supportive and made me feel as if the baby was an essential key to his life. Then to top it off, when I had asked Juelz to go to the abortion clinic with me, he didn't respond to my text. He made me feel as if it was my mistake, and so I had to clean up the mess by myself. Which was true, but a part of me was use to him fixing any significant matters I had encountered, I truly didn't know what to do. In all honesty, a part of me was alone, and unsure of what to do or how to do it. A portion of me was in denial that this wasn't Juelz's child, even after months and me telling KJ this was his baby.

Before being able to respond, he hit me with a low blow. "I have a baby on the way by this girl name Simone. It just happened. I was off so many drugs, and it just happened. She's going to keep the baby. You kept yours. Plus, I'm hurt." He had a look of intended hurt on his face. No tears formed. No pain was present. There was nothing there. I knew Juelz wasn't going to let this go without doing something to get back at me. That wasn't his personality, and as much a player as he proclaimed to be, the man was too emotional for his own good when it came to me. When he was hurt, and especially when I did something, he wanted me to suffer. He would do everything in his power to make sure I felt every inch of pain he felt. Only this time I wasn't hurt. How could I be? I had a child of my own growing inside of me that wasn't his. Truthfully, I was so drained and tired of bullshit and dealing with both these emotional ass men. I didn't even care.

All Juelz had done was make me question his view on love. How could you love a person and know they're going through so much stress within their life, but still make it your goal to attempt to add more scars to the battle wounds that you have given them from being with you and standing by your side previously?

From the look on his face, Juelz had a lot more to tell me. "Simone had gotten pregnant with our first baby in January, right after you told me you were pregnant. But she had lost the baby, and I got her pregnant again two months later." He laughed about the situation, as if I was one of his homies, and he was discussing his latest fuck-up. One baby, I could see as a slip-up. But for him to impregnate this girl right after I announced I was pregnant, that was a new low, even for him. That meant if my baby had been biologically his, he would've continued to have sex with multiple women, more than likely unprotected, which that would've put our child at risk. To top it off, that meant Juelz had already been having sex with this girl before I had told him about the pregnancy. Was he so bitter that he had to try to ruin the only good thing I had in life besides my baby? My joy of being somewhat stress free?

I didn't know what to do, but I knew I couldn't do this anymore. Honestly, I didn't care anymore. Once again, I was back to square one. The only different is I wasn't hurting about his actions. I hoped that Juelz could've put his hurt to the side, realizing what I was going through, and that I needed him to be my support system for once. He needed to think not just about himself, but about those around him who would be affected by his actions. He had to be there for me, like he was there for everyone else, and show a sense of concern. Unfortunately, that was too much. I was so focused on what kind of man I wanted him to be towards me, and stuck on the feeling of his love that I had received during our younger days. I hadn't realized that he wasn't that guy.

Yes, Juelz was there for me, playing with the moving baby inside of my stomach, rubbing, kissing her, and making sure I ate the right foods. But he wasn't there how I wished for him to be. I yearned for a family—and not just a family with anyone, but a family with him. I wanted a family with Juelz, the man I would give up everything for, if I ever had to choose between him and everything else. He didn't see that. All he saw was that I was pregnant by someone named KJ who'd chosen to go against his own child for an outsider. A part of me believed that he was happy KJ wasn't a part of the pregnancy. It felt as if he wanted me to pay for my mistake and the consequences of stepping out on him, even though he did it all the time and there wasn't a real commitment between us. It was life, and sometimes within life, shit just happens.

Here I was again, back where I'd started. Only this time, there was no Juelz, no KJ, and a growing baby inside of me. This time, it felt different, the feeling of loneliness; I felt whenever Juelz up and left, was no longer there. I didn't mind KJ not being there because I didn't hold any real feelings for him after a while—at least, that was what I tried to make myself believe. I couldn't allow myself to show emotions for a man who didn't give a fuck about his child. Not once had he reached out in the last few months to see if I was okay or how the baby was doing. Hell, KJ hadn't even called to see whether our child was growing healthy or not. This baby was nothing to him. I was nothing to him. We meant nothing to him. The crazy thing about it was I felt fine with that; it was best that way. I didn't want my child to have a father who allowed outsiders to disrespect his children, his children's mothers, or would leave their lives because of our disagreements. I wanted a reliable father—a person who, even on bad terms, would never make his child suffer due to his absence.

Even after all of this, I was smiling. Some might think this wasn't a situation to smile over, but one to cry over. I had cried so many nights and prayed for strength to get through everything I had encountered. I had to be strong, not just for me, but for my child.

CHAPTER 14

M onths, some rougher than others, continued to go by and even though it all I still was able to find peace and block out any sense of stress from anyone. My little girl was growing inside of me, day by day. Even though she wasn't here yet, she had already begun to give me a new sense of outlook on this thing called life. My support system wasn't as strong as I would have liked. Which was the reason I kept to myself when I received the news during my second trimester about me having a girl and any other updates within my pregnancy. Unfortunately, I decided to text KJ to tell him the news, and as expected, he called, screaming in my ear, going on about how he knew this was his daughter, and trying to pick out baby names for her. A part of me couldn't see him the same man I once thought he was or even embrace this special moment with him. I knew exactly what he was. His lack of respect for our child made me not even feel comfortable with telling him anything when it came to our child. Which was the reason why I kept the news from him for weeks prior to me reaching out to him, that I received during my second trimester about me having a girl and any other updates within my pregnancy. Another reason for me opting to tell him, was just so I could say, "Hey, I told him." He hadn't been there all this time so I didn't expect his actions too change now.

He had been showing me for months that he didn't give a fuck about his supposedly soon to be first born daughter. I mean, he couldn't have cared about her. His words and actions spoke his true feelings when it came to my child. It was sad enough that I was having a child by a man like this, who I once thought displayed all the signs that I had yearned for Juelz to show me, only to find out that he was just another sorry ass dude out here in the streets that put bitches before his kids.

Don't get it mistaken; I was well aware that we didn't have to be together for both parents to be active in their child's life. We both were free to do whatever we wanted, when we wanted. On the other hand, I knew a child should be raised with both parents in the same household, in order to see their parents show love and affection for each other. Basically, setting the example for them. Teaching them how a man was supposed to treat a woman: with nourishment, love, and care. All this was still possible as long as both parents were able to respect each other and realize that the child was the most important factor in the end. This was the furthest thing from my daughter's reality. KJ wasn't that mature.

It was sad because a child, who had never had the chance to inhale their first real breath of fresh air, could feel so much hatred from a man who was supposed to care for her, protect her, love her, take her to her father-daughter dances, and allow her to feel that love of a father and everything else that came with having an active father. The father-daughter's relationship and a father's love, that was something she would never have or get from him. She would be forced to grow up missing that. It made me despise him even more. He wasn't supposed to allow anyone to disrespect his kids. It shouldn't have mattered who the hell it was. This young bitch had a baby, and I could bet you any kind of money she wasn't about to let him disrespect hers. I was always taught if someone can't respect your kids, then they don't respect you. You never pick an outsider over your children. Hell, you don't even choose family over your children. You stick by your kids and ride for them because at the end of the day, your children are a reflection of you, just as you're a reflection of them.

Thinking about how KJ was still lying next to a bitch who wished death upon his child and said she would harm me with his growing baby inside of me made my blood boil. I had to get off the phone before this boy turned my positive attitude instantly to a negative one. Plus, there was only so much fake excitement I could handle in one day. I cut him off from his rant. "KJ, I've gotta go. Bye." I said, hanging up in his face.

KJ wasn't a little boy, at least not age wise. Immature, yes, but this damn sure wasn't his first run around the block when it came to having children. I knew of two boys. One supposedly lived out of town. As for the other son, by the name of Jake, I'll just say that from the outside looking in, one would think that Jake was his only child, at least the only one he acknowledged. With this not being his first child, and with KJ being nearly forty and me being twenty-three, one would think he knew how to control his women and lay out common rules when it came to his kids and their mothers. This was a man who I had learned never truly cared about his kids, or at least not mines.

I had become use to not having many people around because of my pregnancy.

Mostly, everyone I knew had turned their backs on me. Here I was, pregnant by a man who didn't give a fuck whether the baby died or survived. Juelz, the man whose child I thought I would have carried, had decided to impregnate every female he came in contact with, making me realize that Juelz, genuinely wasn't the best man to have a family with either. He was just someone that I had invested so many years into that I had become attached on the idea as to what could have become from our situation. Although, truthfully there was nothing ever going to come from it. Family wasn't an option due to my mother running KJ's name into the mud without even meeting him. She did not realized that her words would have a bearing on our relationship but also her grandchild.

I knew she didn't want me to have a child and could care less about the child's well-being during the pregnancy. However, I still reached out to tell my mother about the news I had received, since KJ now knew. She wasn't supportive of me at all when it came to my child. I still figured I should tell her. Why not? I'd told KJ, so telling another person who didn't have anything positive to say wasn't going to hurt me.

I didn't expect much—well, nothing positive. She wasn't very supportive or positive when it came to me being pregnant. I was her only daughter, and I figured she wouldn't be as caustic as usual. Boy, was I wrong. I decided to send her a text revealing the news that I was having a girl, figuring maybe this would help spark some excitement in her about my pregnancy. Instead, her response was typical, "What do you want me to say? Congratulations?" No matter how upset or bothered she was by me carrying a child, she wasn't about to ruin my moment. Before I knew it, she was flooding my phone with text messages. I figured that they were probably all negative, given from the first two messages I had read, so I didn't think to open the remaining of her messages. She had a thing with control, and she felt she was supposed to control her kids' lives, especially mine. The moment I disagreed or displayed a sign of independence, she was on the phone telling me off to all of our family members. That was just her. Most people had a parent who stood by their children during hard times. Others had parents who would rather talk about them to others while making things even harder for their children to overcome life's events. Even after all that, I still didn't care. I made a promise that I would never be the same kind of parent she was to me, no matter the situation. She warned me previously about dealing with someone as old as KJ and seen a lot of red flags that I didn't notice and chose to overlook; through everything that KJ had put me through from the fights, prank calls, threats, giving out my address, Niesha issue, and not being active in my pregnancy. I couldn't tell her any of that. I had defended KJ and turned my back on everyone for prejudging him before anyone had even had a chance to meet him, and possibly given him a chance. In reality, all she was attempting to do was prevent me from making some of the same mistakes she possibly made in her past and I was to blind to pay attention. Deep down I was embarrassed and ashamed that my life was such a mess. I couldn't tell her or anyone else about what was going on during my pregnancy. I refused to hear the words "I told you so." Listening was something I wished I would have done back then, but here I was—stuck! There was nothing I could do about it.

CHAPTER 15

This pregnancy was almost over. I was eight months along now and still stress free without a care in the world. Until I checked my bank account. I had gone broke! I was living off of credit cards, robbing Peter to pay Paul. I didn't know what to do. I was waiting on a lump sum of money to come in from when I was in a car crash a few years back, but there wasn't a guaranteed day as to when that would take place.

While most people who were pregnant and placed in unfortunate situations like this would have instantly processed the thought of calling their child's father. Unfortunately, KJ didn't give a flying fuck about me and whether I had enough money to eat or pay my rent. The last time I had spoken to him, he was calling me a bitch and a hoe while screaming, "Fuck you and that baby! Find that baby a daddy. It's me and my new girlfriend that matters!" Honestly, I would have rather been homeless before I asked him for anything.

No matter how bad things were between two parents sharing the same child with each other, you should always feel that regardless of any tension or arguments, deep down you knew that person had your back and your best interests at heart. That wasn't my reality. I had to fend for myself. My family looked at me as if I was the breadwinner, even though my entire family had money. Being broke was something that no one wanted to believe, especially when it came to me. The ones who did believe it simply wanted to hear about it so they could have something to discuss and gossip amongst each other. I would've rather been broke in silence, than to have been broke and the topic of group discussion. My mother was a last option, because I knew she wasn't a big supporter of my decision to keep my child. The questioning that came along with asking her for help wasn't worth it. It wasn't that I couldn't get money or make money. It was the fact that being pregnant had me feeling extremely lazy with me now approaching my delivery date. I had a hundred and one ways on how to get money before there was a child living inside of me. Now that I was pregnant, I had to watch how I moved and with whom I moved with.

I knew one person was going to stand side by side with me: Juelz. At least, I hoped. Months had gone by since we'd last talked, yet here I was, reaching out for him in a time of need for the first time ever…money wise! His baby situation hadn't crossed my mind since that day we last spoke. The matter was out of my control and it was up to him to do what he felt was best for his life. I just needed him to hold me down, for once, within my time of struggle. Luckily for me, Juelz stepped out of his usual "figure it out yourself" character, and came to my rescue without a second thought, for once, financially. He was paying rent when I was short, as well as car notes, insurance and any other bills I threw his way. He helped around the house, asked about doctor's appointments, made sure I was eating all the right foods for the baby, and put money in my pocket. Juelz knew me like the back of his hand, at least when it came to how I moved with money. For me to call and say I was broke, he knew something wasn't right.

Normally, I was the breadwinner, the positive thinker, the motivator, the supporter, and the friend that Juelz needed. It was finally time for him to return the helping hand. Hell, after all the motels, cars, basements, mattresses on the floor, and couches I had slept on and in with him, Juelz owed me that much. Everything wasn't good, but it was manageable. It seemed like it was one bill after another that I couldn't pay, one more thing I had to cry to Juelz about. I wasn't use to asking Juelz for anything; even though we had been dealing with each other for years, doing for each other was not a part of our relationship. Juelz was one of those people who would listen and witness me going through hardship and knowing he could help, but wouldn't. He would rather make me overcome those burdens alone. He was a good listener when it came to hearing my problems, but coming up with the solution—meaning he was going to help—wasn't his thing. Only time Juelz got involved in my problems was if there was a chance it could hit the streets and his homies would hear about it, which would make him look stupid and leave him trying to cover up the matter. Besides that, any situation I faced it was always,

"What did your people say?" or, "That's fucked up," or his favorite, "So what are you going to do?" So, when he came through to help with this situation, I was beyond shocked. I didn't know if it was the fact that his money wasn't as long as mines, or he didn't know how to respond to a lot of situations, or the fact that he was embarrassed to tell me that he didn't have it, or he didn't honestly know how to be there for me. But, the contributions Juelz were making at this very moment were beyond appreciated.

Juelz called morning and night, making sure I was okay. He left his boys to come in early if I wanted to go grocery shopping. He'd wash clothes and did anything that required me lifting, bending or picking up bags, mainly because I had to walk up flights of stairs. He was finally being supportive. Yet, through it all, whenever we were together, something didn't feel right. We weren't together, actually—that would never happen. But he was back to doing the same things he'd done months prior, before our last falling out.

After months of being there and around him constantly, he began to become prideful after a while. I had never needed him for anything, and now that I was at my lowest, when I would ask him to pay for something or required help, he suddenly became rude and nasty by the mouth, as if my problems were not his problems. That was true. They weren't his problems. But when he was homeless, needed somewhere to sleep, couldn't afford to buy himself anything to eat, got shot, and didn't know how he would live from a gunshot wound, that wasn't my problem either. Yet, I stood by his side for everything, and when I mean everything, I mean everything that he allowed me to be by his side for. But, Juelz being Juelz, it was always something new with him. Only this time I didn't know how to interpret the bombshell that he was about to drop on me, and I wasn't sure I could stand by his side anymore, even if I was broke.

"Hey, I have a baby on the way," he said while lying across the living room floor. I sat at my maple wooden table with rocks in the center of it. Before I even had a chance to respond, he continued. "Hell, I know I told you about the last baby, but that girl lost her baby again. There's this other girl, and I feel like since you're having a baby, I might as well have one. I was hurt, so I went crazy." I remained silent because I could tell he wasn't done. "Yeah, she's having a boy …"

His phone rang, and he picked it up to talk to his new baby momma, I assumed, from the nature of the conversation.

"Juelz, get the fuck out. Matter of fact, let me drop you off since you didn't drive."

Looking puzzled, he stood and walked out the door. I slammed the door behind him. He'd better call his new baby momma, whom he'd met the week before, and tell her to come get him or catch a taxi. I wasn't upset about his baby news—that was his problem. It was the disrespect that I wasn't going to allow.

I had known Juelz was a bit childish and spiteful. I simply didn't know his spitefulness was this extreme. I realized I was pregnant by another man. The difference between Juelz and I was that I realized I had made a mistake by even dealing with KJ, and especially by getting pregnant. This was my first time being pregnant, so I overlooked a lot of things that most people saw coming. KJ was the "perfect man," initially, and even once he found out I was pregnant. It wasn't until I was no longer able to get the abortion that KJ showed me that he was a child of the devil, and his mother was Satan's sister. Before I became that far along in the pregnancy, I had asked Juelz to go to the abortion clinic with me, and he basically told me I had to face this entire situation by myself. See, my pregnancy had just happened. It wasn't planned on my end. It was merely just life taking its course. It was obvious that he was not able to get over the fact that I was having another man's child. Well, I didn't care anymore. My baby was almost here, and as he and everyone else could see, I had refused to get rid of my child to please those around me. My pregnancy was no longer an issue—just the people I had around me.

Juelz was that stupid, that he would go out and make a baby just to get even. Word had been buzzing in the street that Juelz had gotten seven girls pregnant, and his excuse always remained "My girl had a baby on me, so I am hurt," when it was bought back to me. I even knew a couple of the girls—not personally, but from around the way. I was never one to listen to the streets when it came to Juelz's stupid ass, especially not when it came to shit like this. Later on, I found out every female who was supposed to have been pregnant by Juelz, was actually pregnant by him. The babies ended up passing due to miscarriages. Juelz was so hurt over life just taking its course with me and a baby coming out of it as the end result, that he decided to have kids with random women, repeatedly? That was on him. He was the one who would have to deal with those women, not me.

That was when it hit me again: Juelz never fucking loved me. What kind of man goes out and gets a numerous of different women pregnant, just to get even?

Then he was blaming me for his multiple baby mommas? He was the one fucking these girls unprotected. Get the fuck out of here. In my pregnancy, I was creating a blessing in the making. Juelz had always begged me for a son. I would've given him his son and any extra kids he wanted after I had my daughter, even though I always said I only wanted one child. Given the amount of love I had for Juelz, there wasn't anything I wouldn't have done for him back then. But I wasn't feeling this shit! I was done with being a damn fool for this man. Juelz basically stood in my face and told me he was having a son with someone else as if it was nothing. He was deranged, and it showed how he thought of me. How he valued himself; most importantly, how he valued his kids.

Juelz was losing it. He was also a handful, and I knew there wasn't another female walking this earth willing to deal with his stubborn and childish ways. Juelz was losing it. The irrational decisions he was deciding to do, while blaming me for the end results were nothing more than excuses. No woman was going to stick around as long as I did and put up with his drama. As far as that baby, it was made because of me, so his new baby momma should've called me to thank me after she called him. I mean, I was the reasoning behind the baby being created, as Juelz stated. In reality, that was bullshit. Juelz had made that baby because that's what he wanted to do. Regardless, if he genuinely didn't want a child with the woman carrying his baby, that wasn't my concern. He was now stuck. What Juelz hadn't realized, was that I would've never had a child by a man who makes childish decisions such as creating a child out of spite. The hurt he was experiencing from my bearing of KJ's child was only the beginning. The feeling of knowing that I would never give him what he always wanted from me, a child, would stick with him for the rest of his life. The bearing of a child with him, no matter how much we spoke on the topic in the past, would never happen, at least not with me.

Putting Juelz out of my house meant that we were no longer talking, and the help that I was receiving was now cut off. That really didn't matter. The nigga was disrespectful, and was starting to become big-headed. I guess he finally had the chance to be the man when it came to the money situation between us, and that moment of power went to his head. He would snap out for no reason at all, and that's when I realized that he realized I needed him. That day, I vowed to never need anyone else in my life if it pertained to my daughter and I. I promised myself I would give Juelz back every dollar he had ever given me. If this was his actions when he had an inch of power, I could only picture how he would become now that he was able to say he'd done things for me. It didn't matter. He was going to receive every dollar back, he had given me. Until then, I had to call my mother to ask her for help, because the first of the month was approaching, which meant my rent money was due.

C HAPTER 16

Finally reaching out to my mother for help with my financial troubles, of course, she wanted to do a family sit-down. Usually, I hated family sit-downs because it was normally your parents doing all the talking, asking a lot of questions, and trying to get all in your business—just to turn around and say that they weren't going to be able to help you or would have to see what they could do for you. Unfortunately, I was too broke to reject any kind of sit-down that had to do with me and my financial situation. As I prepared myself for the long, drawn-out conversation, I decided to face this meeting head-on.

I slipped on a pair of sweatpants and a tank top so that I could rush to my family meeting. My cell phone rang from the kitchen counter. I heard a gentle, firm voice on the other end as I answered. "May I speak to Ebony. I am calling from Solutions of Technology Industry about a position that you were phone interviewed for months ago."

I stared at the phone. This had to be God looking out for me. It was true that God was always there when needed the most, because I didn't recall applying for a job, let alone doing a phone interview. Hell, maybe it was the pregnancy brain kicking in, but I wasn't about to let this opportunity close before it open. I went along with the nice gentleman on the other end of the receiver. I didn't know what the position entailed of, or where the company was located, but as long as it was in the same state as me, I didn't care what or where the job was located.

"Ma'am, after carefully looking over your interview screen and background, we have decided that you're a great fit for our company. HR will be sending you over an offer letter. When it comes to compensation, what is the minimum you are willing to accept?"

I stared at the other end of the receiver in disbelief. This had to be a dream. It took everything in me to hold my composure, to hold back the screams and tears of joy. "Think fast, Ebony," I thought. "Fifty-thousand dollars yearly, due to my level of experience within this field and background." I spoke with confidence and pride. The reality was I didn't know what the position was, but I wanted to see if he would accept my salary request.

"Fifty-thousand sounds reasonable. I will be sure to have HR send you an offer letter over shortly." He responded, without a second thought.

I stood in the middle of my living room, confused about what had just taken place. I couldn't believe this company, which I couldn't even remember applying for and interviewing with, had accepted my request to start with fifty-thousand dollars per year. I was twenty-three years old and making fifty grand. This was amazing!

As I hopped into my truck, all I could do was smile and thank God repeatedly as I pulled out of my driveway and headed over to my family meeting. Because I now had a job, I didn't need my mother's help. Well, I still needed to borrow nine hundred dollars until I received my first check. Besides that, I was good. God had answered my prayers and heard my cries. Thankful was an understatement for how I felt at this moment. I was so excited that I didn't even notice how close I was to my mother's house. Minutes away from the meeting, I couldn't stop smiling. During my entire pregnancy, nothing had gone completely right. Everything bad that could've possibly happened had taken place, from KJ not being there for the baby and saying, "Fuck our child," to me being stuck with a selfish-ass person like KJ as my child's father. With all the bad shit happening because of this pregnancy, I thought God was punishing me for my past mistakes, and that was why he'd sent me KJ. I didn't know what the hell I'd done to deserve such a cowardly man in my life, or why a child who wasn't born into this world yet deserved to have her father repeatedly deny her and not be there for her. It didn't matter, though. This job was exactly what I needed. It was the financial blessing I had been praying for. It was time to get back on my feet, and no one could ruin that but me.

I pulled into my mother's driveway and sat in my car for an extra five minutes, thanking God and soaking in the wonderful news that had just taken place. My mother must have seen me pull into her driveway because she called my car phone and asked, "What's taking you so long to come up?"

I responded with a simple, "Here I come," while getting out of the car. The door was already ajar.

"Ebony, what's the plan? How are you broke? Did you pay off your car?" The questions flew towards me before I had gotten a chance to catch my breath from walking from my car to the front door.

"Um, you know I am almost nine months pregnant, right? I just had to walk from the car to the front door. Let me sit down first, and then I'll answer your questions. As a matter of fact, what's here to eat? Did you cook? As for the plan, I just need nine hundred dollars, and I'll pay you back when I get paid. I totally forgot to tell you, I got hired for some IT company. Can you check my e-mail and look over what HR sent me?" Requesting as I kicked off my tennis shoes.

"You got a job? Where? When? What's the position? Did you tell them that you were pregnant?" My mother asked with a puzzled look on her face.

"Of course not. I am legally not required to disclose to them that I am pregnant. Secondly, I am not exactly sure as to where the job is located or the position I will be filling. I just know it's a job, and that is something I don't have at the current moment. Can you check my e-mail so that we both can learn what the position is?" I yelled as I walked into the kitchen to raid the refrigerator.

"Ebony? This is a contracting job! You make fifty-thousand? You're twenty-five thousand short of me? That's great money! Oh, something came in the mail for you. I think it has something to do with that money you've been waiting for," she said with a sense of excitement in her voice. I had never heard my mother have a conversation with me and speak as if she had an inch of pride in me since I had become pregnant. I only heard her speak positive of me on special occasions, when she was one-on-one with someone and I eavesdropped prior to me announcing my pregnancy to her. This was something new to me.

I shuffled through the mail that set on the dining room table until coming across a thick envelope with my name on it, as well as the word "Allstate Insurance Claims." I ripped opened the letter and pulled out a thick packet filled with numerous documents in reference to my claim decision. As I scanned through each page, I noticed a paragraph that stated I would be receiving eighty-thousand as the lump sum of money, and I was due to receive it within the next few days, in the form of a check. This time I didn't scream. I simply placed my hands over my face and cried. So many blessings had come my way, and all within twenty-four hours. There was nothing that could ruin this moment. I rushed to e-mail HR back the signed acceptance letter to their job offer, and just like that I was due to start work the following week.

C HAPTER 17

Today was my first day on the job. I arrived in the parking lot bright and early at 8:30 a.m. on Monday morning. I knew early morning activities and myself didn't mix, so I made sure to set my alarm to 6:45 am so I'd have more than enough time to get to work. First impressions were everything. Given the old, wrinkled white guy who had just pulled up on the side of me in his 2005 Honda Accord, I was signaling some unwanted attention to myself. I didn't know whether it was my car, or the fact that a young African American woman was driving a foreign car. I didn't know what his deal was, but I could feel him eagle-eyeing me almost as if he was discombobulated for some odd reason. I didn't have time for this shit. I was tired, hungry, and extremely exhausted from being pregnant. This little girl inside of me was the reason for me having the appetite of six people. I needed a before breakfast snack while I waited for breakfast most days. This imbecile parked on the side of me wouldn't have been prepared for the words that would have come out of this pregnant, hungry lady's mouth. I didn't have enough time to stop and get breakfast, and this baby was not happy about it at all.

After an extra fifteen minutes of prepping myself in the car for the long day ahead of me, I decided to gather my things and head toward the tan building that stood in front of me.

Literally, I hadn't even gotten a chance to sit down in my new office, before Bri filled my phone with screenshots, then called screaming at the top of her lungs. That was one thing I could say: nothing got past Bri unnoticed, not a lick of shade or tea. She was the "Screenshot Queen." In the process of attempting to get Bri to settle down so I could make out exactly what she was seeking to tell me before reading her text messages, here came Tiara, my little cousin, flooding my phone with screenshots about a post Raven had made on social media towards KJ and me. It had all made sense now. This most likely had to be the reasoning to what Bri was blabbering about on the other end of the phone. As Bri was just finishing informing me about Raven's social media post after she finally calmed down, Tiara had sent me a number of screen shots of the comments being made.

Family was family, but when it came to these bottom feeders, the word "family" was used loosely. I logged on to Bri's Facebook page and went completely off. It didn't require me to make multiple comments to ruffle these little girls' feathers. All Raven had to do was call me like a grown woman and ask me, or tell me what was up with her and KJ. That was what I would've done. I didn't see why she even cared. She was supposedly in love with a young guy who looked as if he was every bit of fifteen and Raven was twenty-five—and she just so happened to pin a baby on him. It wasn't my job to figure it out if the baby was his, because I didn't care.

Normally, I wouldn't have gone back and forth with them, they weren't worth the energy. But, after all the craziness that had taken place within my life due to this pregnancy with Juelz and KJ, I needed a laugh or two. If Raven wanted KJ so badly, then we could have traded places easily, if it was possible. KJ was no trophy or anything worth beefing over. Even though I hadn't talked to KJ for some time, he would still call private, call from different numbers, follow my car, sit outside my house, and watch me go inside my house some nights. He'd tell bitches where I lived, have his forty-five-year-old sister send high school threats, and his despicable mother cosigned all the bullshit. If Raven wanted to beef with me over him, then she was definitely barking up the wrong tree and making miserable ass social media posts about the wrong person. I hoped she kept her baby Chihuahuas who were on the post cosigning her stupidity around her at all times. I mean, someone was going to have to be her eyes for when she had to fight off all the different bitches who came from dealing with KJ. Since KJ meant so much to her and was worth beefing with her cousin over, all because she had a crush on him and I wasn't even aware that they even knew each other, then she could have him. It was that easy, problem solved! Facebook was the last thing I wanted to be stressed about. I made one response to the post from Bri's page and kept it moving.

Even though this was my first day, I had to leave early to attend an ultrasound appointment. At my last ultrasound appointment, the doctor had noticed that my daughter only had two vessel cords instead of three. I had to be seen more frequently to make sure that my child was growing and receiving her nutrients, making my pregnancy a high-risk pregnancy. I informed KJ of the matter when I first found out via text, and of course, he didn't care. Regardless of how he might have felt about me, he needed to realize that he'd begged for this child, and so the least he could do was act as if he cared for it. I couldn't make him be something to her that he'd never had in his life before, for example, like being a good father.

I gathered my things and told my coworker that I was going to be out of the office for the remainder of the day due to medical reasoning. This was my first day, but these appointments were mandatory. As I walked to my car, I had just thought about how far I had come. At one point, I was fighting for a man to love me who didn't deserve my love, and I was lost about how I'd become pregnant by a man who I had thought was the perfect man, and he turned out to be the worst. Then my back was against the wall with no support. Now, I was starting a new job and was not acknowledging past relationships and past mistakes. God had blessed me, and He had to break me down in order for me to become the woman I needed to be. I had to remove the people from around me who were weighing me down mentally, physically and emotionally. Boy, did my load feel lighter!

I got in my car and continued to smile. I appreciated what I was truly able to see, what was happening before me. It was worthy of smiling and being thankful for. I decided to drive all the way to my appointment, bumping Kirk Franklin's new song, "Smile."

Upon arrival to my ultrasound appointment, just like any other appointment, I checked in at the front desk, and the nurse requested for me to come to the back to check my vitals. Afterwards, I was taken to the ultrasound room and awaited the doctor. It was the same routine I had been doing once a week for the last few weeks. This ultrasound was precisely like my previous ultrasounds had been, at least that's what I figured.

CHAPTER 18

Bri was still flooding my phone with screenshots. Just as I was getting ready to open her messages, the doctor walked into the room to start my ultrasound procedure. After she put everything in place, we began, and I heard my daughter's heartbeat and saw her little arms and legs.

Then the doctor spoke. "Ma'am, I have news for you. You are going to have to go into labor right now."

I stared at her with confusion, as if this was a joke. I wasn't having any contractions. I wasn't dilating or anything of that sort. "Excuse me?" I spoke, as I reached for the white towel to wipe the cold, blue ultrasound gel off my stomach.

"Ebony, your baby hasn't grown a lot since the last time we saw you. I am going to call over to labor and delivery, to let them know that you're on your way."

Unclear as to what had taken place within those short moments, I didn't feel as if I was going into labor. I wasn't experiencing any pain, and I was still up and moving. She elaborated on her urgent concern about my child's growth by referencing that, "Most babies weigh in at about 5 to 6 pounds during the last term of their mother's pregnancy. You're due to turn nine months in a day or so; while your child is weighing in at only 4 pounds. I am not saying that anything is wrong with your child, I want to make sure that your baby is ok and healthy," said the doctor using a cautionary tone.

I stood there uneasy with the information. "Okay. I have to stop by my house to grab a few things for the baby. I'll be there shortly," were the only words I could find to express my thoughts within this moments.

I was completely nervous. I was about to go into labor! I wasn't afraid but was in shock that this was about to take place. It felt so surreal. I rushed to my car and headed home to get some items. When I arrived home, I paced back and forth through the house, trying to get an understanding as to what was about to happen. I wasn't real big on calling family to tell them my business, but I had to tell someone. I called my cousin Chantel, I figured she'd know what to say and give me some pointers, since she had a child of her own.

It was the basic pep talk. "There's nothing to be scared of. Just do what you have to do." Our conversation lasted no longer than three minutes. She was right: I had to do what I had to do. I took another shower, grabbed a few things, and headed to the hospital.

I wasn't sure as to what happened along the way, or whether I was procrastinating on actually being induced. I could have sworn I was on my way to the hospital, yet I ended up in line at a fast food restaurant. Sad, I know, but I couldn't go into labor on an empty stomach! I arrived at the hospital at 5:08 p.m. From there, I was rushed to Labor and Delivery, located on the south side of the hospital, and placed in a room. From there, it was a waiting game. I laid there in the hospital bed, surfing the web for random things to keep my mind off the fact that I was in labor without any pain.

My doctor, Dr. Jackson, came into the room to check my cervix and see whether I was dilated. He informed me that everything was going to be just fine, considering the fact that I wasn't even an inch dilated. From there, Dr. Jackson inserted this clear ball-like object inside me, which would induce labor. I remained there, inside my hospital room continuously surfing the web, until there was a knocking on the door from the nurse informing me that I had visitors: my mother and uncle. The receptionist at the front desk of this department had me fill out a contact form in case of emergency. I completed the requested document by placing my mother as my emergency contact. I didn't know at that very moment she would be contacting my mother without informing me. A million thoughts had begun to form in my mind as I continued to wait. I hadn't thought to text or call anyone once I was actually in my hospital room, grateful for the receptionist kind gesture to place the phone call. Especially, since on the outside, it looked as if I was dealing with this matter just fine, but deep down I was terrified.

Right after my mother and uncle made themselves comfortable, surprisingly,

Juelz had sent over a text asking, how was the baby doing? With a frank response to his question, "I am in labor."

That was the crazy part about Juelz and me; regardless of whatever we did to each other and how much we tried to leave each other, we always found ourselves back where we started—back in each other's lives.

My uncle and mother sat with me for hours, until finally I felt my first contraction. Honestly, the contractions weren't as bad as I thought they would have been. My contractions started at fifteen minutes apart. I was not requesting an epidural or any pain medicines just yet. I took every inch of the slightest pain while continuing to text Juelz. With my mother and uncle being there, of course the news spread fast throughout the family that I was in labor. I started receiving many calls and texts, but I did not respond to anyone but Juelz. However, Tiara must have gotten wind of me being in labor because she decided that it was her duty to message KJ informing him that I was in labor and what hospital I was in.

Truthfully, I preferred for him not to be there for our daughter's delivery. He hadn't been there for anything else when it came to our child, but I knew my cousin had no idea as to what had taken place during my pregnancy between KJ and I. She was only trying to make sure that he was aware of the arrival of his child. What she didn't know was that KJ wasn't as graceful or excited for the delivery of our child as she thought he would've been. Because moments later, I decided to scroll through social media, and lord behold, KJ had gone on Juelz's social media account logged in under his sister's account, commenting on a picture I was tagged in with Juelz that we'd taken months ago saying, "Oh, I am happy she found someone so she could finally leave me the fuck alone—her and that baby." Here I was in labor, and KJ was on social media commenting on another man's page instead of trying to be a part of his child's birth. More and more, he gave me a reason to dislike him. I made Juelz aware of the comment, and all he could say was, "Fuck dude, he's a clown." That was exactly what he was—a clown. I decided to place a visitors restriction on my room so that no one would be able to visit me or my child without them knowing the passcode to get pass security. Also, I requested the nurse to not allow any calls to come through to my room. KJ was aware that I was in labor and was known for popping up, and I refused to experience any kind of negativity, especially while I was in labor. I didn't need it. I just wanted to have my child and hold her for the first time.

KJ's mother called up to the hospital, trying to seek information to confirm that I was actually in labor. She was as messy as her son. Of course, no information was given to her. I felt it was her fault for him being the way he was. She hadn't raised her son to be a man; she hadn't properly groomed him. Hell, she was barely properly groomed herself. She was the definition of an older woman trying to stay young. Any bullshit that KJ did, she knew about it and condoned it. Hell, he told her everything, so in my eyes, she wasn't any better than him.

Hours had gone by. Juelz excited and cheerful of my delivery. He texted repeatedly nonstop asking, "Is my baby here yet?" He was texting and calling with so much eagerness and concern. He decided that he would stop by the hospital to officially meet my daughter once she was delivered. My contractions had started coming back to back more frequently and intensely. "Where's the nurse?" I screamed while hitting the emergency button that was within arm reach of my bed.

The nurse came running into the room. "Ma'am, what's wrong?" The brown puffy-haired lady asked.

"I need my epidural now!" I said, panicking as another contraction came, causing tears to form in my eyes.

"Okay, ma'am. Let me get the waiver for you to sign. Basically, it's informing you of what could possibly go wrong with an epidural. By time I come back, I will have another nurse ready to take you to get your epidural." She rushed out the room and down the hallway. Within seconds, she came back with the waiver for me to sign.

Usually, I read everything before I sign it. Hell, most of the time I would read the same document multiple times to make sure I didn't miss the small print. But today, my mother had to summarize what the consent form stated. Once I got the "okay" that it was ok to sign the consent form, quickly I signed the waiver to receive my epidural without a thought. I handed it off to the nurse while screaming for my epidural right now.

God had been on my side so much lately, because immediately after, in walked a male nurse with a wheelchair to take me down the hall for my epidural. From the new room, he proceeded to help me out of the wheelchair and onto the bed. Then he opened the back of my gown and inserted the long needle into my spine, releasing the epidural. He left the needle in place for only a minute or two, just long enough to insert a skinny, flexible catheter the size of pencil lead into the epidural space. The process itself felt as if someone had pinched my skin. It was painless and smoothed the slight pain that had instantly turned sharp within moments, had now become bearable. My contraction pain had now become suitable. Now, it was back to playing the waiting game for my cervix to dilate to ten centimeters. My cell phone died, making the hours pass by slower and slower. I had only reached eight centimeters, by the time the clock struck 8:12 am the following morning.

Finally, after hours waiting, the doctor came back into the room to check my cervix again, letting me know that I had reached ten centimeters. It was time to push! They transferred me into another room that was more private, to prepare for the delivery of my child. I was surrounded by doctors from every angle encouraging me to push when instructed. Initially, I thought Dr. Jackson, who was my OB/GYN, was going to deliver this baby of mines. Instead, a doctor by the name of Dr. Perry, who worked on the same team as my OB/GYN, informed me that she would be the primary doctor during the delivery. I liked Dr. Perry. I didn't know whether it was because she was about to help me deliver this baby, or whether it was the fact that she was a successful sister, but I liked her.

"Ebony, I am going to remove the clear ball that Dr. Jackson inserted into your cervix. I am going to need you to scoot down and open your legs for me." She placed a cover over my lower body so I wouldn't be completely exposed. Without a question or remark, I did what she requested. I was ready to get this pregnancy over with, to get this child out of me. Most importantly, I wanted to meet my daughter, hold her tiny fingers, and lay her upon my chest. That very moment was when I realized I was ready. I was ready to be a mother. I was ready to experience unconditional love. I was ready to give unconditional love back. I was ready to release my seed into this big world to watch her blossom into a beautiful flower. I was ready to be a parent.

"Ebony, I need you to give me two big pushes on the count of three, okay? One… Two…Three…Push!" The doctor demanded while trying to get a clear visual of the baby. For some reason, as soon as I started pushing, it felt as if the epidural wore off. The pain I felt now wasn't from contractions. It felt as if I was stopped up, as if I was experiencing fecal impaction. "Ebony, you did great with your last two pushes. Let's try this again. Give me two more," Dr. Perry, forcefully demanded.

I gave her two more big pushes on the count of three, draining all the energy from me. Prompt and assertive with the delivery of this baby, the doctor urged me to give her two more pushes. At this moment, I just couldn't do it. I didn't have the strength or energy in me to deliver this child. Dr. Perry, along with the rest of the medical team, continued rooting for me to continue to push as hard as I could. "I know exactly how many pushes I can do. Just catch my damn baby!" I yelled, legs pinned open with sweating dripping down my face.

I was pushing as hard as I could until I finally heard, "There's the head." I was motivated to get this baby out of me and gave one big push with all the energy I had left in me, making the baby's shoulders come out. Dr. Perry was still rooting and encouraging me to do one more push. Tired, defeated, dehydrated, exhausted, and restless, I found an inch of energy left in me to push once more, and just like that, Winter was born.

My body worn out and exhausted, I collapsed backward towards the hospital bed, as tears rolled down my cheeks. I couldn't believe I had just done it. I had just delivered my daughter. "Give me my daughter," I murmured, as the nurse washed my baby girl's body clean on the other side of the room. I knew the delivery room was packed, but what I hadn't noticed was my mother was in the room, along with so many other people that I didn't recognize.

"Bring me my child," I spoke, with tears continuously flowing down my face as the room full of strangers being to surround my bed as the nurse begin to walk towards me.

"Ebony, here you go, ma'am. You have a beautiful, healthy baby girl weighing four pounds and eight ounces, born at 12:19 p.m. at exactly 37 weeks. Would you like to do the golden hour? This is where your baby naked body is placed upon your chest the first hour she is born. This is the initial bonding time for the baby and mother." As she had begun to place my daughter underneath the gown I wore.

As my precious baby girl laid on my chest so comfortably, it was at this moment I realized all she was all that mattered. I was going to be the person whom she looked up to. The person to teach her life lessons by telling her about some of the adventures and hardship I encountered within my life. I hadn't exactly accomplished any of my long-term goals, but as long as I hadn't given up, I knew that my daughter would grow up being proud of her mother. I was going to continue to pursue my degree, working a new job, and now that I had welcomed a beautiful baby girl into the world, at least I had accomplished my goal to get back on track. Regardless of how much stress and discomfort I endured within my pregnancy, it didn't matter at this moment. All that mattered was being the best parent to my baby girl. My beautiful baby girl Winter was all that mattered.

Years of my life had gone by due to me focusing on trying to get Juelz to love me unconditionally. At this very moment, I truly accepted and realized Juelz wasn't the man for me. We just weren't meant to be. The more I allowed him to be in my life, the more he would continue to come around without ever being the man I wanted him to be. At this turning point within my life, I refused to accept anything or anyone that didn't show the consistency or respect needed to be shown towards me as a person, woman, and mother. The kind of relationship that Juelz and I shared wasn't healthy, and truthfully, it would not have been healthy for my child as well. Her love was all the love I needed. A smaller version of me to love me unconditionally, just as much as I would love her. This was the love I had been searching for, the fulfillment that I had needed. She was what made me complete. She would be the reason for me becoming a stronger woman. She was the reason behind me feeling tingly inside, with a constant smile. There wasn't any amount of drama that I went through to ever make me think about replacing her. Weird as it may sound, all the drama, pain and emotional distress was worth it. Initially, I was afraid, but it wasn't about being a parent or raising a child. I was afraid of losing the fairytale that had once dreamed of with Juelz, someone who really wasn't even worth having a fairytale with. Honestly, after all that had taken place, I could admit to myself that deep down inside I didn't believe I truly ever wanted a child with Juelz. I was just so stuck on our past and history that we shared that I overlooked the fact that if I truly wanted to genuinely have a child with him, I would have shared a child with him years ago. It was the contentment that we shared and my comfort level with him that kept me near. It was now time for me to grow, not just as a person, but as a woman. It was time for me to experience my life without Juelz. It was time for me to experience life without living in the fairytale land that I had created within my head; it was time for me to focus on self love. It was time for me to face my reality. I had embarrassed myself long enough by allowing my value to be lowered, all from being attached to someone so childish and full of drama. I had become in love with the thought of being in love with Juelz and him loving me back. When in reality I lost my self along the way trying to mold Juelz into the man I wanted him to be. This caused me to ignore and overlook all the signs that we were never going to be anything more than what we already were. The longer I allowed him to be around, the longer he was going to continue to be around doing exactly what he had been doing for years…nothing, just wasting years.

It took me meeting KJ, and going through all the drama and bullshit with him, to finally open my eyes enough to leave a toxic relationship and actually give birth to my daughter to understand that God places certain people in your life to help you sometimes get a clearer picture of the people that you're allowing into your life, your comfort zone, and your level of peace. This allows you to open your eyes to see who really has your best interest and who's just here blocking you from seeing your true worth. If I continued on this path, it would only me be making a fool of myself. Especially when it was right in front of me that, it wasn't meant to be. No matter how much I didn't care for KJ, I was thankful for him giving me my daughter, my best friend, a part of me that would always be here to represent me. At the end of the day, Winter was worth it all. The situation shaped and molded me without me realizing it. I would have never been able to be the best parent possible to my daughter if I continually tried to make Juelz, who really wasn't shit, into this perfect man or consider why KJ couldn't love his kids. It wasn't worth the time or energy…they weren't worth the time or energy. Winter was my blessing. I was a mother, and I was more than thankful—I was blessed! Finally, I truly understood what mattered in life and what didn't. Winter was what mattered. Showering her with love and helping her become a stronger, wiser woman than her mother was my only goal.